Toddler Invasion

Scott frowned and shook his head to clear it. One part of his brain was telling him to close his eyes and ignore the children in his yard. They were figments of his imagination that would soon go away. Another part of his brain was trying to rouse him, to warn him that his territory was being invaded, that it was time to rise and defend his land from interlopers.

He moved restlessly, not sure which impulse to follow.

Then he heard a shout. This time the voice was adult, and it came from the neighboring yard.

Scott waited, sure the owner of the voice would appear out of nowhere, just as the children had.

A figure slipped into his yard. This one was definitely no child. This one had all the rounded attributes of a full-grown woman.

Dear Reader:

Happy New Year! Now that the holiday rush is through you can sit down, kick off your shoes and open the cover of a Silhouette Desire.

As you might know, we'll be continuing the *Man of the Month* program through 1990. In the upcoming year look for men created by some of your favorite authors: Elizabeth Lowell, Annette Broadrick, Diana Palmer, Nancy Martin and Ann Major. Also, we'll be presenting Barbara Boswell's first-Desire-ever as a *Man of the Month*.

But Desire is more than the *Man of the Month*. Each and every book is a wonderful love story in which the emotional and the sensual go hand-in-hand. The book can be humorous or serious, but it will always be satisfying.

So whether you're a first-time reader or a regular, welcome to Desire 1990—I know you're going to be pleased.

Lucia Macro
Senior Editor

RAYE MORGAN

TOO MANY BABIES

SILHOUETTE *Desire*

Published by Silhouette Books New York

America's Publisher of Contemporary Romance

SILHOUETTE BOOKS
300 East 42nd St., New York, N.Y. 10017

ISBN: 0-373-05543-9

First Silhouette Books printing January 1990

Printed in the U.S.A.

RAYE MORGAN

favors settings in the west, which is where she has spent most of her life. She admits to a penchant for western heros, believing that whether he's a rugged outdoorsman or a smooth city sophisticate he tends to have a streak of wildness that the romantic heroine can't resist taming. She's been married to one of those western men for twenty years and is busy raising four more in her Southern California home.

One

Scott Bradley wasn't expecting intruders—especially not ghostly figures in white nightclothes. So when his backyard was invaded, at first he didn't trust his own eyesight.

It was close to midnight. He'd come in late on an international flight with an interminable layover in Bombay. Sitting in the cockpit of the giant jet airliner, all he'd thought about for the last two thousand miles was how good it was going to feel to soak away his tiredness in his own backyard hot tub.

He made the short hop from Los Angeles to Palm Springs and drove his Porsche from the airport to the home kept ever-ready by his wonderful daily housekeeper, Rebecca. Sighing happily, he took off his uniform, then went right out back, leaving the lights off, and slipping into the water. Lying against the side, he gazed up at the star-studded desert sky. He closed his eyes, feeling all the tension begin to ooze out into the hot water, and he sighed again. This was the life. His body was still vibrating from the long flight. He needed this, badly. Groggy from lack of sleep, he began to drowse.

And then for some reason he opened his eyes and something white and fleeting caught his attention. He squinted, looking into the darkness at the end of his yard opposite from his pool. Something moved, then came into full focus for a moment. It seemed to be a girl with long blond hair, dressed in flowing, translucent white. He blinked, and the vision was gone.

"Good Lord," he muttered to himself. "I must really be beat this time." He was thankful he'd forgone the stiff drink he'd thought about having. Better to see ghostly little girls than pink elephants. He began to sink back down, eyelids drifting shut.

But no, there she was again, this time shimmying up his tree, her gown fluttering in the breeze. He frowned. That was his tree, wasn't it? Some kind of fruit tree. Apricot, maybe. He never paid any attention to it, letting the gardener take the fruit he wanted, and throwing out the rest. And now it contained one ghostly little girl. Unless he was seeing things.

His gaze sharpened and he tried to wake up enough to concentrate. Something told him this was no vision. Visions didn't eat apricots. This had to be a real little girl.

Suddenly there was another child, a towheaded boy built like a fireplug, also in white. The child stopped and gazed about the yard and Scott could have sworn his eyes gleamed with an unearthly light. Then he, too, disappeared, only to reappear shimmying up the tree.

Scott frowned and shook his head to clear it. One part of his brain was telling him to close his eyes and ignore the children—they were figments of his imagination that would soon go away. Another part of his brain was trying to rouse him, to warn him his territory was being invaded, that it was time to rise and defend his land from interlopers.

He moved restlessly in the water, not sure which impulse to follow, and then there was a third child. This one moved on terribly unsteady legs still bowed. And this one saw him.

Standing very still, dressed only in diapers, the newcomer lifted a chubby hand and pointed at him. "Aga doo," the toddler seemed to say.

"Beanie!" cried a voice from the tree. "Go home! Go home now!"

"Aga doo," the youngest repeated, starting toward the tree on wobbly legs.

Scott sighed. There was no use kidding himself, no use hoping this was all a desert mirage. What it was, was a toddler invasion. He was going to have to rouse himself to do something about it. Any minute now.

"Beanie."

This time the voice was adult and coming from the neighboring yard. Scott's head swivelled and he waited, sure the owner of the voice would appear out of nowhere, just as the others had.

"Beanie, where are you, you little rascal?"

Scott sat very still and watched, fascinated, as the bottom end of a plank in the fence shared by the two yards rose like one side of a teeter-totter and another ghostly figure slipped into the yard.

This one was definitely no child. Dressed in white gauzy baby doll pajamas the like of which he hadn't seen since his teenage fantasies, this one had all the rounded attributes of a full-grown woman. Silver-blond hair curled in ringlets down her back. The pretty, heart-shaped face was creased with a worried look as she gazed about the yard.

"Beanie?" she called out. "Where are you?"

Scott realized, suddenly, that he was holding his breath. He could see all of them now, the two in the tree, the young one hovering at the bottom, the lovely woman searching for them. Each wore white and each seemed to be glowing somehow. The thought that they were supernatural flickered through his mind again, but he dismissed it quickly. He was fully awake now, and fully aware that they were all too real.

"Beanie!" She'd found the baby and scooped him up into her arms. "You bad boy. Coming over here barefoot! Who knows what awful things this man has in his yard?" She peered up into the tree. "Beth! Barnaby! You two get down this instant! You're supposed to be in bed and you know it!"

"Mommy, we're just getting apricots. The man doesn't want them."

She shifted the baby from one hip to the other with the practiced ease of a longtime mom. "Well, that's true. How anyone can let good food rot...."

"He's a mean old man," the young voice answered. "The kids down the street told me. He's a mean old man and he hates kids."

"Mean old man," a male version of the voice echoed from the treetop.

Scott found the urge to defend himself rising in his chest. Mean, maybe—but old at thirty-eight? Hardly! It was time to assert his authority in the situation. He looked about for his towel and found it hanging almost close enough to reach.

"If he doesn't like kids," the woman was saying, "it's just as well he's never home, isn't it?"

"Where is he, Mommy? Where does he go?"

The baby chose that moment to glare at Scott again, lift his little hand and point, yelling "Aga! Aga!" But no one paid any attention.

His mother merely shifted him a bit on her hip and went on talking up into the tree to her other children. "I don't know, honey. April didn't tell me. On trips, I guess." She reached her free arm up to help the little boy down. "Come on, Beth. You've got so many apricots in that nightgown, you won't be able to walk."

"I hope he doesn't come back while we're staying in April's house. I hope he never comes back. I hope—"

Scott had taken just about all the verbal abuse he was ready to take. He wasn't used to being called mean and being shunned.

"Guess what," he said in a deep, loud voice, surging up out of the water and reaching for the oversize towel at the same time. "It's too late for hoping. He's already back." He whipped the towel around his dark, naked body and pulled it tightly around his hips. "Now would you like to explain just exactly what all you people are doing in my yard?"

That was as far as he got. For mere fractions of a second the four intruders stood transfixed, shocked by his presence. Then they swung into action.

The woman screamed. The little girl screamed. The little boy screamed, and so did the baby. Caught up in the moment, Scott almost screamed himself. Still shrieking, the neighbors ran for the fence. The woman shoved the baby through, then the other two children, before slipping through herself, screaming all the while.

"Hey," he yelled, going after them, frowning in annoyance at all the noise they were making. Half the city must have heard them by now. "You could at least apologize."

He reached the fence and leaned over it, watching them run for the house next door, the woman carrying the baby and stopping to help the little boy. The little girl was the straggler, looking back and calling to her mother in a broken voice, "Mommy, I dropped all my apricots!"

Pangs of guilt shot through him. After all, what had they been doing that was all that bad? Just eating fruit he didn't bother with himself. Was that so terrible?

He looked down. Apricots covered the ground at his feet. He reached down and picked a couple of them up. "Hey, kid," he called over the fence. "Here. Catch." He tossed two nice big apricots to the girl.

Instead of reaching out to capture them, she screamed again. "Mommy! He's throwing things!"

Scott shook his head, aghast. "No, I—"

Too late. The woman had whirled and was bearing down on him. "Listen, mister," she stormed as she neared where he stood. "I know we were trespassing. I'll make sure it doesn't happen again. But it was a harmless thing we did. And for a grown man to stand there and throw things at a child!"

"No, really," Scott said, trying to smile. She was close now, and even in the moonlight, he could see that she was a very pretty young woman. Pretty women usually liked him. Women in general, in fact, usually fell all over him. Surely once he'd explained....

"I wasn't throwing them *at* her. I was throwing them *to* her. You do see the difference, don't you?" He gave her the "we adults understand these things" look and shrugged charmingly, expecting to see that familiar little glint appear in her gaze, to see the line around the mouth soften, the lips begin to turn up at the corners.

Unfortunately, those things didn't happen. Instead, she put her hands on her hips, facing him as though he were a barking dog and she a mama cat protecting a basketful of kittens. The hard line around her mouth tightened. Her blue eyes flashed unfriendly fire.

"I've heard about you, mister," she told him evenly. "You lay a finger on any one of my children and I'll make sure you're sorry for it."

Scott would have liked to have pursued the topic. He'd never made any bones about the fact that he liked his privacy, that he would prefer to live among adults in a place where the patter of little feet was not often heard. But he wasn't the boogie man. This reputation for hating kids seemed to be getting out of hand.

But before he could begin his own defense, a sound came from the house. Everyone turned toward it. Easy enough to identify, it seemed to strike each one of them with the same sense of horror.

"Babies," Scott said, staring at the pretty woman. "More babies." He quickly counted the three still outside. The sound coming from the house indicated at least two more. "How many kids do you have, lady?" he asked incredulously.

Her eyes shone with defiance. "As many as I want, mister," she replied. But she began to back away toward the house.

"Wait." As horrifying as the prospect of even more children was, he found he didn't want to lose her so quickly.

She hesitated. "What is it?"

For a long moment, all he could do was look at her. The back light from the house was illuminating her, showing off her trim waist, rounded hips, and the full, dark-tipped breasts. The baby doll pajamas were practically transparent. Her wild silver hair flew about her face like an enchanted mist, and her long, slender legs ended in fluffy white bedroom slippers, completing a picture that was sending his senses into a tailspin. Common sense was tugging on his consciousness, trying to remind him that with all these children, there must be a father about somewhere.

"I . . . listen, couldn't we start over here? I didn't mean to scare you and the kids."

Her blue eyes were wary, cynical. "No? Then what exactly did you mean to do?"

He shrugged disarmingly, but ignored the question. "I'd like to get to know you better," he said with the smooth tone of a practiced charmer. "After you get those little . . . those kids to bed, why don't you come on over for a nightcap?" The husband problem nagged at him. After all, babies didn't usually appear on doorsteps these days. There was always a father involved, at least at the onset. "You and your husband," he added hastily. "After all, we're neighbors. We should talk." He smiled.

She didn't. "Sorry mister," she replied evenly. "I teach my children not to talk to strangers. They learn best by example."

With a flick of her hair, she turned and strode quickly to the sliding glass door where her children were waiting. Scott watched her disappear, drawing the drapes behind her. He sighed, feeling strangely lonely all of a sudden.

Turning back to his own dark house, he started across the lawn, and quickly realized why the woman in the baby doll pajamas had been scathing about his yard. Against his tender bare feet, the grass seemed to have turned into a field of jagged rocks and lethal stickle burrs.

"Ow, ow, ow," he muttered in agony as he made his way gingerly across it. When he reached the patio, he bent down to pull out a few burrs, at the same time grabbing at the towel that kept sliding off his backside and swearing under his breath. Compared to this hostile hellhole he called home, Bombay was beginning to seem downright attractive.

Things looked a little different in the morning as Scott sat and drank his orange juice and gazed out at the shiny blue desert sky with not a cloud in sight. The night before had been unusual, but hardly devastating. True, there were a lot of kids around. But it wasn't the memories of crying children that haunted him. Memories of their mother were much more vivid.

He wasn't sure what it was exactly that had captivated his imagination. She was awfully pretty, with a body that could melt stone, but then, so were a lot of women—women without children attached.

He made a face at his cold cereal. Children. There was nothing worse. Sticky fingers. Whiny voices. He'd spent a good part of his life very carefully staying away from the little rug rats. And now they were invading his territory.

He'd never actually made it a rule not to date women with children. It had just sort of turned out that way. In his line of work, most of the women he met were unattached. None of them wanted children any more than he did. At least, he supposed that was true. Come to think of it, the subject had never come up.

He looked out through the window at the red tile roof of the house next door, wondering if she were up yet. Funny he'd never noticed her before. She must have moved in while he was flying somewhere in another corner of the world.

He had a vivid picture of the woman who had been living there lately. Dark, pretty in an over-obvious way. The sort of woman who dressed as though she were heading for a cocktail lounge at nine in the morning. Not his type, but attractive enough. He'd said "hello" now and again, but that was about the extent of it. He hadn't been particularly intrigued.

This new one was different. Despite the children, she interested him. Now that he thought of it, he really ought to make amends. After all, he had scared the poor kids half to death when he'd leapt up out of the hot tub. He'd made them drop their apricots.

His gaze lowered to the heavily laden branches of his apricot tree. That was it. He would take them a bowl of apricots.

A few minutes later he was on his way to his neighbor's front door, a large canister of apricots in hand. Just being neighborly.

Two

Cathy Feenstra stared down at the three identical cribs holding three nearly identical six-month-old babies. For once, all three were asleep at the same time. She stood very still. The last thing in the world she wanted to do was wake them. She examined them slowly, from the dark wisps of hair on the top of their little round heads to their perfect tiny fingernails. So very much alike. It was amazing.

Two of them were girls, and one was a boy. Their names were Michelle, Robert and Kimberly, but Cathy and her crew had taken to calling them Pink, Blue and Daffodil. Yellow just hadn't struck quite the same note.

"Poor little babies," she whispered at last. "I wish I knew where your mama is."

Daffodil sighed in her sleep, as though she were in heartfelt agreement. Cathy smiled. "Don't worry, little one," she murmured. "One way or another, we'll find her. I promise you that."

Things that tore families apart fired up a fierce anger in Cathy—things like mothers disappearing, fathers walking out. Was it naive to want an intact family unit with all the nurturing love that it could hold for every child? Probably. But she couldn't help it. She still longed for that in the same way children longed for a white Christmas. It was just the way things should be.

Turning away from the three, she backed carefully out of the room. Easing the door closed, she almost tripped over Beanie, her own barely walking tyke in diapers. She scooped him up with a practiced hand and started down the stairs.

"Mama." Beth was at the bottom, looking up, her strawberry-blond hair tied back in a crooked braid, her wise six-going-on-thirty face slightly anxious. "Are the babies asleep?"

Cathy nodded wearily. "Finally." Reaching the bottom of the stairs, she gave Beanie a noisy kiss and set him down. "Now, at last I've got some time for my own brood. What do you children want for breakfast?"

"Mama." Beth clasped her hands behind her back and looked self-conscious. "I...I already fixed something for us."

Cathy turned to stare at her daughter. "Why you little darling! What did you fix?"

Beth's smile wavered as though she wasn't sure if she'd done something good or something that only made things worse. "Toast with butter and honey. And milk."

Cathy felt one level of tension flowing out of her, and at the same time, tears welled in her eyes. Ever since Joey had left them, she'd been strung so tightly, trying to hold it all together. There were days when the effort seemed too much to bear. But there was always Beth, like a gift. What had she done to deserve such a daughter?

"You angel!" She reached out and gave her child a big bear hug. "Thank you so much." Her voice cracked just a little and she blinked hard to get rid of the tears. "You're such a help. I don't know what I'd do without you."

Beth looked so pleased it brought a lump to Cathy's throat. She smiled at her daughter as she brushed the hair out of her eyes. She hadn't been paying enough attention to her little girl. If she didn't watch out, she'd turn around and find Beth grown up. She gave her daughter another hug and released her, standing back to look at her with motherly love and pride.

She still didn't understand how a man could turn his back on a child like this. That Joey had left his largely imperfect wife for greener pastures was no great surprise. But that he could have looked into Beth's trusting sea-green eyes and turned and walked away was incomprehensible to her.

"Joey, my boy," she murmured to herself, "you don't know what you're missing."

"Mommy, Mommy!" The shriek was Barnaby's and it came from the sidewalk where he was riding his bike. "The mean man's coming!"

Cathy and Beth froze, staring at each other.

Barnaby ran through the front door as though the devil were chasing him, his red hair standing out from his head. "The mean man!" he cried as he threw himself against his mother, his chubby arms clutching her knees.

Before Cathy had time to react, Scott was leaning on the door jamb, smiling rather sheepishly. "Hello. Your local 'mean man' is here, in the flesh. May I come in?"

Cathy hardly knew what to say. Could this really be the same jerk who'd frightened her children the night before? Some nerve he had.

Scott seemed to read the outrage in her eyes. He stepped into the entry and went on quickly. "I brought a peace offering. See?" He held out the canister, filled to the rim with fat, ripe apricots. "And I promise not to do one mean thing while I'm here."

Cathy hesitated, her gaze going from his smiling dark eyes to the apricots he held and back to his eyes again. For some reason, she almost felt like smiling back at him. It must be that he just had that kind of face. She bit her lip instead. "You won't throw things at the children?" she asked tartly.

"I didn't..." He flushed and stopped, refusing to demean himself by going into an explanation. "Let's start fresh, shall we? I'm Scott Bradley." He stuck out a large hand.

She stared at it for a moment, then took it, feeling her own hand disappearing in the strength of his. "I'm Cathy Feenstra. And these are Beth, Barnaby and Beanie." She pulled her hand away from his before he was quite ready to release it. "My three children."

He nodded coolly at the kids and turned back to Cathy immediately, a move she noted with cynicism. She was used to judging a man by how he responded to her children. She hadn't met many who'd passed her test.

She was getting a better look at him than she'd had the night before. Then, with the moon casting a faint light across his angular face and his hairy naked chest, he'd seemed like some monster of the night, a reincarnation of Dracula. Here in the light of day, in slacks and a polo shirt, he looked very different. His dark hair was neatly combed, and his dark eyes glinted with a friendly light. His shoulders were wide, his arms muscular. Noticing the way the polo shirt clung to the rounded hardness of his chest and revealed the bulge of his biceps, she felt a tiny shiver of awareness, something she hadn't felt in so long that she'd almost forgotten such feelings existed. Reason enough to keep the man at arm's length, she thought grimly.

While she was examining him, he was examining her room with a wary glance, one eyebrow raised. "Aren't there more?" he asked.

Pretending not to know what he was talking about, she made her eyes wide and innocent. "More what?"

He said the "b" word as though it were almost obscene. "Babies."

She smiled. "I only have three children."

"But last night . . ."

Let him stew, she thought. He was certainly easy to tease. And he deserved a little teasing after last night. Completely ignoring his uneasiness, she smiled again. "Thank you so much for the apricots. May I offer you a cup of coffee?"

He frowned, looking about suspiciously, as though he were afraid some tiny tot might pounce on him at any moment if he lowered his guard. "Thanks," he said slowly. "That would be nice."

"Please sit down." She indicated the plush furniture in the living room. "I'll be right back."

She retreated into the kitchen. Beth was right behind her, carrying the apricots.

"He was nice to bring these to us," Beth said, setting the canister down on the table. "Be nice to him, Mom."

Cathy turned to stare at her oldest child. "I'm nice to everyone," she said with forced cheer as she pulled a coffee mug down off the rack and filled it with hot liquid.

Beth shook her head. "Uh-uh. Not to men."

Cathy leaned against the counter for a moment, closing her eyes, knowing Beth was absolutely right. Not to men. Not since Joey, her husband and the father of her three children had said so long one day and left without a backward glance. It had been over a year since they'd heard from him, except for the divorce papers. But it could have been yesterday.

Pulling herself together, she managed a smile. "I'll try harder, pumpkin," she said softly. "Honest. Starting right now."

Beth still looked worried. "Mom, he's cute."

She got out the cream and a bowl of sugar. "Cute doesn't cut it in this world of ours. Didn't you hear your brother? He's a mean man."

Beth shook her head wisely. "No, Mom. I don't think he's mean. I think he's nice." Her eyes were very big and earnest as she added, "We need a dad around here. I like him."

Cathy swung around, horrified. "Beth!"

"He's cute," she insisted stubbornly.

"Let me give you a word of advice, young lady. Don't pick your man for 'cute.' There are a lot more important things in this world. Don't find out the hard way." *Like I did* was implicit in her silence. That was as close as she'd ever come to criticizing their father in front of the children and she quickly retreated from the edge of that cliff. They deserved to have good memories of their father. That was something she would never take away from them.

She put everything onto a lacquer tray and started for the living room. "Come on," she said. "Let's go be nice."

Scott was sitting in the living room wondering why he'd come. There were two children staring at him. One was hiding behind the velveteen-covered chair, peering from around the side as though Scott were surely the enemy. The other was sitting at his feet, looking him over with unabashed curiosity, touching him now and then with one chubby finger, then drawing it back and gurgling happily.

He looked up with relief when the women reentered the room and he immediately jumped up to help Cathy with the tray.

"Thank you," she said, and, about to say something back, he looked down into her eyes.

They were huge and blue and there was a mystery there that caught at him, throwing him off base and making him forget what he'd been about to say. Instead, he stood where he was and stared at her a little too long, until she said, "Is something wrong?"

"No," he said quickly, feeling like a fool. He slumped down onto the couch again, trying hard to regain his usual savoir faire. Every time he looked at her he was more and more intrigued. What was it about this woman that was doing this to him?

Her silver-blond hair shimmered around her shoulders like sunlight and her rosebud mouth looked sexy and kissable and her long, tanned legs looked gorgeous in those short shorts. But hey, come on. It was nothing he hadn't seen before.

And yet . . . and yet . . .

There was something about this woman that tugged at something within him.

"Is your . . . husband around?" he asked, then winced at his obviousness. Still, he had to know and she certainly hadn't been forthcoming on the issue.

"No," she said, glancing quickly at the children. "He's not."

"Oh." Well, that didn't help much, did it?

She got up to let Barnaby outside, and he craned his neck to look at her hand. She wasn't wearing any jewelry at all, so he still couldn't be certain. He tried to formulate another way of asking more specifically, but before he could find the words, the little girl spoke.

"Our daddy's gone," she said matter-of-factly. "Mommy isn't married anymore."

"Beth!" Cathy gazed at her daughter in perplexed horror as she came back to sit down. She'd never known Beth to be so forward before. This missing daddy thing was bothering her more than she'd realized if her little girl was ready to throw her mother into the arms of the first decent-looking man to walk through the front door.

Beth shrugged, looking apologetically at her mother. "It's true," she said softly, burying her face on her mother's shoulder.

Cathy looked at Scott, her arms around her daughter. She wanted to turn cold and brush him off, but somehow she couldn't force it. There was an openness about the man, a warmth she seemed to automatically respond to, as though she'd known him for a long time. She felt an instinctive trust, though why that was, she couldn't imagine.

She'd promised her daughter she would try to be nice to Scott, and to tell the truth, that was turning out to be easier to do than she had thought. Maybe they could be friends. Wouldn't that be nice? But friendship required honesty. She had to be very clear on where things stood.

"I'm divorced," she admitted, her blue eyes wide and honest. She patted Beth and set her free. "And I'm very busy raising my three children on my own. I have absolutely no time for anything else."

For one of the few times in his life, Scott was embarrassed. Suddenly he saw how this whole scene was playing itself out. How could he sit here and ask her these things so crudely, right in front of the kids? What an idiot. He might as well grin and say, "Hey babe, like your bod. Are you free to join me in a short, fun-filled affair? No strings attached, honest. And say, leave the kids at home, okay?" Like some self-centered swinger at a singles' bar. He was seeing himself in an unfamiliar mirror and it was not a pretty picture.

But before he'd thought of a way to redeem himself, a sound came from upstairs. Everyone froze.

Scott looked toward the stairway. "What is that?" he asked carefully.

Cathy tried to look innocent but her smile was a delicious declaration of guilt. "What is what?" she responded, blinking her lovely blue eyes.

The sound came louder, the wailing unmistakable. The first voice had now been joined by another. Scott turned on her accusingly. "Now don't try to con me. I'm not hearing things. You've got more babies upstairs." The "b" word again. He seemed to wince as he said it.

Cathy laughed and sighed with mock discouragement. "Oh gee, can't put anything over on you, can I?" she teased, rising from her chair. She hesitated for a moment, glancing at Beanie. It had been apparent for a few moments now that his diaper needed changing. But the babies' cries were getting louder. Beanie would have to wait.

"You'll have to excuse me," she told Scott. "I'll just go see what the little darlings want."

"I'll go, too," Beth said, running to catch up with her mother. In a moment, they were both gone.

Scott was all alone again. All alone, except for the toddler who sat at his feet and watched every move he made, completely absorbed. Scott stared down into the huge baby-blue eyes. Beanie stared back.

"Hi, kid," Scott said at last.

Beanie stared.

"You need your diaper changed," Scott noted reluctantly. "Don't you?"

A beatific smile appeared on the chubby little face. "Aga doo," he agreed, bouncing his arms.

Scott's sigh was deep and heartfelt. He raised his eyes to the heavens. "Why me?" he muttered. "Didn't I do enough of this? Haven't I served my time?"

Nobody answered and he rose, looking around for fresh diapers. There was a stack of white, fluffy ones on a side chair. He grabbed a cotton blanket from the floor and laid it out on the couch, then scooped Beanie up and gently put him down on his back on the blanket.

"Hold on, partner," he murmured to the child. "This will only take a minute."

He pulled out the pins and took Beanie by the feet, easily lifting him out of the diaper and using the cloth to clean the little bottom at the same time.

"Just like riding a bicycle," he said caustically as he worked. "It's a talent you never lose."

Still holding Beanie up, he flicked in the clean diaper, using one hand to press in the folds. In no time, the child was changed and the dirty diaper was stowed away in the diaper pail in the hallway.

Scott found a bathroom and rinsed off his hands, and then he was back in the living room again, sitting on the couch, with Beanie at his feet, now watching him with even stronger adoration.

"Aga," the tot murmured.

"Aga yourself," Scott said back. "Why don't you go find some nice dirt to play in?"

Beanie merely gurgled and took hold of Scott's pant leg with his wet hand. Scott watched, his face squinting in distaste.

The crying upstairs had stopped and in a moment, Cathy reappeared. She took in the two of them and reached down to pull her baby up into her arms. "Now to change you," she began, but then she frowned and patted his bottom with the touch of an expert. "I thought..." She held him out and looked at him, then shrugged, obviously deciding she must have been mistaken. Scott sat watching, not saying a word. After all, two could play the teasing game.

Cathy looked at him suspiciously. There was something about that twinkle in his eyes...

"Everything okay upstairs?" he asked, all inno-
cence.

She sat down, Beanie in her lap. "Yes. Beth is singing to them."

He nodded, watching her. "How many of 'them'
are there, exactly?"

She stared at him. "You don't know?" she asked at
last.

He was confused. "Know what?"

Beth had appeared on the landing. Cathy looked up,
then set Beanie on his little bowed legs and called,
"Beth, would you please take Beanie with you? You
two can watch TV in my bedroom, okay?"

Scott could tell she wanted to get the children out of
the way so that they could talk frankly, so he waited
with her while Beanie negotiated the stairs and disappeared from sight with Beth. As soon as they were
gone, Cathy rose from her chair and came over to sit
beside him on the couch, a move he considered definitely propitious.

She brought a scent with her, a mixture of orange
blossoms and soap. It washed over him as she sat
down, turning her head so that her hair whipped past
his face. He almost reached out and touched it. She
was close now and looking at him conspiratorially, but
all he could think of was how pink and full her lips
were, how smooth and creamy her skin was. Her arms
were bare like her legs. He wanted to touch her, make
sure she was real. But when his gaze finally rose to
meet hers, he had all the proof he needed.

The blue eyes chilled the air between them in a hurry. "Finished?" she snapped.

"Are you serious?" he responded without missing a beat, his dark eyes laughing at her. He put an arm across the back of the couch and she very deliberately turned to keep herself well away from it.

She sighed, looking at his handsome face. She couldn't deny to herself that his scrutiny was exciting, that she had felt a seductive shiver as his gaze had lingered here and there. But she wasn't about to admit it to him.

"I didn't get rid of the children so that we could fool around," she told him evenly. "If I've given you the wrong impression, I'm sorry. I didn't want them to hear some of the things I'm going to ask you. And believe me, those things have nothing to do with your love life."

"Darn," he said faintly, but he waited for her to go on.

"How much," she said, watching his reaction intently, "do you know about April Meadows?"

The name didn't ring a bell. "Who?"

Her shoulders sagged. "You mean you don't know her at all? She's your neighbor. She lives in this house." She frowned. "I can't believe you don't know her. After all, you got to know me quickly enough."

Scott was becoming more and more confused. "Wait a minute. Who is this April Meadows? There's been a brunette living here for about a year."

Cathy nodded. "That's her."

"But we never did more than nod and say hello."

Cathy made a face of disbelief, putting Scott on the defensive.

"She wasn't my type," he protested.

Their eyes met and the question hung between them almost involuntarily—am I your type?

Scott grinned and answered it, though it had not been stated aloud. "Absolutely," he said.

Cathy flushed and tried to hold back the smile that was rising in her. "We're getting off the subject," she said tartly, as much to hold herself in check as to hold him. "The fact is, this is April Meadows's house, and those three babies upstairs are hers, too. I don't really live here. But she's gone. And I'm trying to find her." She waited a moment to let that sink in.

"You mean those three little babies were abandoned by their mother?" Despite the way he felt about children, that shocked him.

Cathy hesitated. "Well, I'd hate to go that far just yet," she said. "I'm sure there's a logical explanation for her disappearance. If I could only figure out what it is. Now tell me everything you know about her."

He shrugged. "Like I said, I don't really know her. Maybe one of the other neighbors..."

Cathy shook her head. "I've asked all up and down the street. I can't believe how people can live within breathing distance of one another and not know one thing about each other's lives! It's amazing. Everyone's noticed her, but no one knows anything about her."

Scott nodded slowly, but his mind was on other things she'd said earlier. "Could we backtrack a little? If you don't live here, what exactly are you doing here? What is your connection to this woman?"

"Okay. I've known April slightly for about six months, ever since the triplets were born."

"Triplets." The word stuck in his throat. "Three little mirror images?"

Cathy nodded. "Almost. They're beauties. I can't believe you've never seen them, living right next door."

He swallowed hard. The concept of triplets boggled his mind. "I'm gone a lot."

"So I've heard. Anyway, I do babysitting to help make ends meet, and April hires me now and then to watch her little ones. This time she was going out of town so she asked if I could stay with them all weekend. I arrived Friday night, waved goodbye to April, and haven't seen or heard from her since."

"It's Wednesday."

"I know. She was supposed to be back Sunday night." Cathy sighed. "I have no idea where she is. She was very mysterious about it. She was going to call me Friday night to give me the number of where she was staying. No call. Nothing."

His dark gaze became thoughtful. "You think something happened to her?"

She hesitated. "I don't know," she said slowly. "That's what I thought at first. I called hospitals in the area to check on accidents. But I don't really know where she was headed, so that was pretty useless."

Scott shrugged. "There must be someone you can call. A grandmother. An employer."

Cathy shook her head. "I've searched the house from top to bottom. There are no names, no addresses anywhere. As I said, I've gone up and down the street asking neighbors. No one knows a thing about this woman."

"Where does she work?"

"You got me. She never told me."

Scott leaned back and thought for a moment, then shrugged again. "I guess you'll have to call the police," he said.

Cathy took a deep breath and let it out slowly. "I—I don't want to do that," she said, looking at Scott and wondering why she felt safe telling him things she was telling no one else. "There's something about April. I've always had the feeling she was, well, not doing anything illegal necessarily, but skating close to the edge. Do you know what I mean?"

He nodded slowly, searching her eyes. "But so what? That's not your problem. And neither are her kids."

She twisted her hands together, wondering how she was going to explain this to him. "I don't quite feel that way. These little babies are so adorable. I can't bear to think of them being tossed around by some government agency, put in God-knows-what kind of institutional environment. I can take better care of them than any agency can. Until April shows up again."

He had to admire her commitment, even if it sounded foolhardy to him. "I think you're crazy. But if you're willing to do it, stay." His gaze took in her frown and he thought to himself that her staying was the best thing that could happen for him.

"Okay," she said haltingly, her eyes wide as she stared into his. "There's one more thing that makes that a bit risky."

Her eyes really knocked him out. He'd never seen such vivid blue before. He'd seen diamonds with less sparkle. A lock of silver-blond hair tumbled down over one eye and he wanted to brush it aside, to keep it from obstructing his view of all that blue. A man could drown in those eyes, take a plunge into eternity. What a way to go.

"What's that?" he asked, trying to keep his mind on what she was saying, but feeling a bit breathless. "What's the problem?"

"I've been getting these telephone calls. Some man keeps insisting I know where April is and threatening to show up in person if I don't tell him where she can be found."

It sounded like a spurned lover to Scott. But then, what did he know? He was having a hard time thinking logically at the moment. Cathy's scent was going to his head like the rush of strong brandy. He moved closer to her on the couch, almost involuntarily drawn, as though she'd cast a spell on him that he couldn't shake. "I...I could stay here with you," he proposed. "Would that help?"

She made a move as though to get back the distance between them, but somehow she never quite finished it. "Stay here?" she repeated blankly. "What for?"

"I don't know. Protection." He leaned closer. The thought of protecting her was making him feel strong and manly. There was a vague sense of the ridiculous flitting in the back of his mind, trying to tell him he was sinking into absurdity here, but he ignored it. Enjoying her was feeling so very good.

"Protection?" Her eyes widened.

"Sure," he murmured. His arm left the back of the couch and his hand dropped to her shoulder. "I could stay here to make sure nothing happened to you. Or the kids."

She blinked, as though she'd just noticed how really close he was. But she didn't move away. Instead, her gaze dropped to his mouth. This was it. He could feel it. She was just too delightful to resist.

This was going to be the kiss that stopped history in its tracks. She looked so good. He felt so tender. The moment was right, and he was going to put their relationship on a whole new footing. He moved in for the kill, sliding toward her across the couch, leaning forward, reaching with his hands...

It wasn't until his face hit the pillow that he really believed she'd escaped. Somehow she'd managed to wriggle away before he'd trapped her, leaving him grasping at empty air.

She was quick, he'd give her that. He straightened slowly, gazing reproachfully at where she stood above him, tapping her foot.

"Thank you for dropping by, Mr. Bradley," she said, turning to stride for the door. "It is getting late, isn't it?'' She flung open the door and stood back, hands on her hips, waiting for him to leave.

Scott came toward her slowly, not sure how they'd swung so quickly from possibilities to flat denial. "I didn't mean to scare you," he began.

"Scare me?" Her eyes blazed. This man had another think coming if he thought she scared so easily. "No, Mr. Bradley. You didn't scare me. What you did was tempt me. Like that serpent in the Garden of Eden holding out the apple. What I'm doing is turning it down." She gestured for him to leave. "So nice to have met you. Thank you for the apricots."

"Cathy..."

She smiled as she waved him out the door and closed it behind him. But the smile faded as soon as he was out of sight, and she sank against the cold, hard wood, staring into space. How was it possible that a strange man could affect her like this? He was right. He had scared her a bit. It was irritating to think she had come close to losing perspective so easily. She would have to be more careful in the future.

Carelessness was what had always gotten her into trouble. She'd married Joey on the spur of the moment, swept off her feet by the handsome baseball player just on the verge of signing a major league contract. She'd had Beth and Barnaby, the twins, right away, so sure that Joey would love them the way she did, that it would cement their marriage with love and happiness. Instead, it had torn them apart, especially when Beanie had come along, a surprise to them both. The children she'd thought of as symbols of their love had been burdens to Joey. As far as he was concerned, they just got in the way.

If she'd been more careful, she would have realized the truth. She'd learned her lesson. She was careful now. Every move was thought out. She would never take for granted again that someone she loved would look at the world the way she did. She would never take love for granted, either. Love was supreme carelessness. It was just too dangerous to risk.

The annoying buzz of the telephone split the air. She opened her eyes and stared at it, dreading it, letting it ring. But then she began to make her way slowly toward it. After all, April could be at the other end of the line. She couldn't take the risk of missing her.

Three

_____

She took the receiver in her hand and hesitated before putting it to her ear. "Hello?"

A rasping sigh of exasperation was her answer. "It's you again, isn't it? Listen, lady, I've had enough of your runaround. Where's April?" He'd sounded from the first like some gangland hood.

Cathy had had about enough; she'd told him over and over that April was missing. She put on a phony telephone operator voice and said shrilly. "To whom did you wish to speak, sir?"

"You know damn well who I want to talk to."

"Sorry. There is no one here by that name. Please try again on some other occasion." With a flourish, she replaced the phone in its cradle.

Staring at it, she willed it not to ring again. Hadn't he learned by now that he wasn't going to get anything out of her?

She jumped when the phone sounded, and then she sighed. This man was her albatross, it seemed. Resigned, she picked up the phone. "Hello," she said sadly.

His voice was strained and harsh. "Don't play games with me, lady. You know what I want. If I don't get it, right now, I'm going to come over there and terrorize you a little."

That was exactly what she was most afraid of. Yelling at her over the phone was one thing. Coming over and yelling at her in front of her children was quite another. Her fingers curled more tightly around the plastic receiver. "Listen. I don't mean to play games with you, but if you'd just stop making these phone calls, I would stop acting silly."

"I'm not making these phone calls for my health, lady. I want April."

Cathy closed her eyes and nodded. "So do I, mister. You don't know how badly I want her back."

"Don't give me that. You know where she is. She wouldn't go off and leave those three brats with you not knowing."

"Well, that's just what she did do. Tell you what. If you find her, let me know where she is, okay?"

Her caller didn't enjoy her little joke. His voice got softer, but at the same time more menacing. "Lady, I guess I am going to have to pay you a visit."

Cathy's throat was suddenly dry. This was just what she wanted to avoid. "Who...who are you... exactly?"

"You'll see when I get there."

She swallowed, her gaze darting about the room, seeking salvation—or at least a good idea.

"I think I ought to warn you," she said quickly. "My next door neighbor is a cop." She picked up the entire phone and lugged it to the open sliding glass door. Luck was with her. Scott was watering his yard. "There he is now," she hissed into the receiver. "Hi!" she called, pulling open the screen door and waving merrily. "Hi, Officer Bradley," she added. "You going to be around today?"

Very near the fence that separated their yards, Scott glared across at her. "Where would I go?" he called back.

"Great," she responded loudly. "I may need you. Stay in touch."

Ignoring Scott's startled look, she drew back into the house. "You see?" she hissed into the phone. "I've got the police at my beck and call. You'd better keep away from here."

"That cop can't be with you all the time, lady. The time will come when he's looking the other way. And then...watch out!"

The dial tone buzzed in her ear. "I will watch out for you, you slime ball," she muttered as she put the telephone back where it belonged. She turned nervously, anxious to do something but unsure of what she could possibly do to remedy this mess that was brewing. One thing was becoming clear. She was going to have to go and find April. The woman had to be somewhere. Maybe if she went looking for her, she'd find something out.

"I'll give you until tomorrow morning, April Meadows," she murmured, clasping her hands together, her blue eyes troubled. "Then I move."

Scott stared after her long after she'd disappeared into the house again. Water ran through his plants, puddling in all the wrong places, and he barely noticed. He was fully involved in trying to explain to himself what had just happened.

The woman had kicked him out of her house not ten minutes before. Now she was yoo-hooing from the place, telling him to stay in touch because she might need him. Need him? He shook his head.

No, this situation was definitely poison. He'd never wanted to get domestic, and that was the word that most perfectly described Cathy Feenstra. Domestic. He made a face.

Babies didn't mix with the Scott Bradley lifestyle. Never had, never would. It was funny how attractive he'd found Cathy, all the same. So attractive, in fact, he hadn't been able to keep his hands off her. The look of her, the scent of her clean body was suddenly in his head and he shook it to rid himself of the wave of sensation that accompanied it.

Trying to kiss her had been a big mistake. He didn't need a woman like that. Especially when she didn't seem to know herself what she wanted. One minute it

was "Never darken my door again," the next it was
"Stick around, I may need you." No, she had to be
nuts. A little unbalanced. That did it. He turned off
the hose and rolled it back on the wheel with the air of
a man who'd made up his mind.

Yes, that did it. She was awfully cute, but she was
definitely air conditioned between the ears. And she
had too many babies, anyway.

Time to get real here. He knew what his problem
was. It had been too long since he'd had the proper
sort of female companionship. All he had to do was
get out his little black book, pick a number, and his
troubles would be over. He chuckled to himself as he
went into the house. Yes, that was all he needed.

The first obstacle to initiating his new plan was
finding the little black book. It wasn't next to the
telephone, nor in the drawer with his checks and re-
ceipts. He looked in the liquor cabinet, beside the
breadbox in the kitchen, and in his dresser drawers.
No black book. When he sat down and tried to think
where he might have left it last, the memories were
vague. It had been an awfully long time since he'd
used that book.

It finally turned up at the back of his gardening
cabinet. He got a warm feeling just holding it in his
hand, turning it, feeling the soft leather. Ah, his little
black book. How many wonderful evenings had
started with it?

Sitting down by the telephone, he began to thumb
through it. Funny, he thought right away, how unfamiliar some of the names were. There weren't many

that he could even assign faces to. But here was a beauty. Carol Lane. A redhead with a great sense of humor, as he remembered. He dialed her number.

"Scott, is that really you? It's been ages!"

She sounded as redheaded as ever and they chatted for a few minutes. This was more like it. This was the way women usually responded.

"I know this is short notice," Scott said at last. "But I was wondering if you would like to join me for dinner tonight. We could try to rekindle some old flames."

"Dinner?" Her voice changed all of a sudden. "Scott, don't you remember? I got married last summer."

That was just the beginning. Jennifer Garvey's roommate informed Scott that she was trekking in the Himalayas and had fallen in love with a goatherd. Julie Brown was now Julie Bartok. When he called Florie Manning, a vocabularyless child answered and he hung up without waiting to find out more.

Finally he sat very still and stared sadly at his beloved black book. What was wrong with everyone? And why hadn't he noticed when this change had come over them all?

When he thought back over the last year he began to get an inkling of where things had gone wrong. How often had he come back from a trip and spent the weekend reading and watching sports on TV instead of getting out and mixing with the singles crowd? His biggest mistake had been getting involved with that mountain climbing group. The adventures in Sierra

Nevada had been a lot of fun, but not too many women had wanted to come along. He'd let himself get out of touch. Now it was going to take real effort to get back into the swim of things.

Effort paid off. After another half hour of calling, he found Tawny Spires willing to join him for dinner. He vaguely remembered her as a slinky femme fatale he'd met at a New Year's Eve party. But she seemed to remember him more clearly.

"I'll be there at seven," she promised breathlessly. "With bells on."

Bells he could do without, but he spent the rest of the afternoon happily preparing for her visit. Steaks on the barbecue, he thought. Twilight by the side of his swimming pool, golden wine glistening in crystal goblets as the sun went down in the desert sky. A little mood music to set the tone.

Tawny arrived right on time. She was tall and pretty and dressed in a low-cut purple dress. Scott let her in and smiled and said all the right things, then wondered why he'd invited her.

"Oooh, your house is so nice," she gushed. "I just love rocks. Where did you find all these rocks?"

His smile was strained as he took his rare piece of Burmese jade from her hands and put it back in the case where it belonged. "Minerals," he said evenly. "They're not rocks. They're minerals."

"Do you go rock collecting a lot? I just love theme picnics."

He frowned. Was there really a brain inside that pretty head? "I collected most of these minerals all over the world, from dealers," he told her. "They aren't the sort of thing you just find lying around these days."

She nodded happily. "I'm a collector, too. I collect matchbook covers. I've got matchbooks from every bar in San Diego and I've got a good start on Riverside County." She smiled blissfully. "I spent a whole lot of time collecting."

"I'm impressed."

"Most people are. Would you like to see it sometime?"

He was just a bit confused. "See what?" he asked suspiciously.

She blinked vacantly. "My matchbook collection. I've got them all pasted up on poster board. It's truly awesome."

He nodded dully. "I guess there are a lot of bars in Riverside County, huh?"

"You better believe it."

Somehow the evening was beginning to stretch out long and painfully before him. But he was determined to have a good time, if only to prove to himself that he didn't need someone like Cathy Feenstra in his life.

He led Tawny out into the backyard. He'd hooked up his radio and speakers to flood the yard with soft music and he'd strewn gardenias in the pool. The coals were warming in the barbecue. The champagne was chilling in an ice bucket. Tawny took it all in at a glance and said, "I hope you don't have mosquitoes."

Scott felt like snarling at that point, but he held himself in check. He found himself starting to turn toward the neighbor's house and he stopped that, too. Instead, he took Tawny's purse, set it inside the door and led her by the hand to the patio loveseat over-looking the shimmering waters of the pool. He was going to enjoy the evening if it killed him.

They sat, they sipped champagne, and he tried to develop a conversation. But it turned out Tawny con-sidered herself a woman of action, not words.

"Let's dance," she said impatiently, right in the middle of a sentence of his regarding the beauty of the evening. She jumped up, switched the radio station to dance music and began a seductive hootchy-kootch before Scott's eyes. "Come on, honey," she cried. "Let's see you move!"

Scott couldn't help it. His first reaction was to glance next door. Sure enough, there was a young face at one of the upstairs windows.

"Stop," he told Tawny, moving quickly to block the view of her frenzied dance. He'd never seen anything so grotesque in his life. Had this sort of thing turned him on once upon a time? Unbelievable. "You can't do that here. There are children next door."

"Children!" She grimaced and sagged to a dispir-ited stop. "Then let's go inside."

"No." He switched the station back to soft music. "No, I have everything set up out here. You sit down. I'll start the steaks."

She flopped down and he put the meat on the grill. This wasn't working and he knew why. He still had

Cathy Feenstra and those kids of hers on his mind. He had to erase them totally. That was the only answer. Mind control. He could do it if he tried.

He stared at the wall. Mind control. Concentration. He could do it—make his mind totally blank where Cathy and the children were concerned.

Suddenly one of the babies began to cry. The windows upstairs were open and the sound came down upon them like a steady breeze from hell.

"There's a baby crying." Tawny looked at him accusingly.

Steady. Mind control. Concentration. "Pay no attention." He dropped down beside her and forced himself to smile. He would not look at Cathy's house again, no matter what. "Now, where were we?"

Tawny tried to smile back but it was obvious that something was bothering her. "Now there are two babies crying," she informed him, as though he couldn't hear for himself. "Why can't they close the windows or something?" She twisted nervously in her seat. "Can you call the police about babies crying? I mean isn't that disturbing the peace or something?"

"Ignore it," he advised. "If you don't let it into your mind, it isn't happening. Listen to the music."

Tawny made the attempt for three or four seconds, then sighed. It was just too hard for her. "I think there are three babies crying now," she said sadly, her fingers tangled together in a knot. "It's getting louder and louder. I just can't stand it. Can't we go inside or something?"

Temptation was strong to look at Cathy's house, but Scott was standing firm.

"You can't give in to this sort of thing," he told her sternly, not realizing he was speaking mostly to himself. "You've got to make your mind strong. You've got to keep control."

"Listen. I don't like babies. I don't like to be reminded of babies. Tell you what. Let's go get a drink somewhere adult."

He shook his head. "That would be giving in," he said stoutly. "We'll stay right here and fight this thing."

Tawny was looking over his shoulder and suddenly her eyes widened with horror. "Now there's one on the roof. Can you believe it? The nerve of some people!"

Scott's hands were clenched in white-knuckled fists; he was forcing himself not to turn around. "Ignore it," he ground out through clenched teeth. "Don't pay any attention."

But Tawny seemed captivated and repelled. "Your neighbors are crazy. Why would they let a baby play on the roof like that? What if he fell or something?"

Scott made a strangled sound.

She looked at him, then back at the house next door. Exasperated, she shrugged. "Oh well, at least he's not one of the ones who's crying." She sighed. "I just hope the kid makes it. That's all. It looks dangerous to me."

"Aga doo," came a little voice floating in over the music.

Suddenly stricken, Scott whirled. Beanie was on the roof of the garage, about ten feet away from the open window he must have crawled out of. He was on the edge of a flat part of the roof, just inches from the slippery slope. In the seconds that Scott stared, horrified, Cathy was out the window and beginning a careful climb out on the roof toward the baby.

Forgetting all his resolutions, he flew to the fence. "Cathy, wait."

She glanced down at him and shook her head. There was a white line around her mouth, but she was trying to remain calm. "No, listen, I can handle this," she reassured him, her voice shaking. "You go on back to your—" she glanced at Tawny and her eyes widened ever so slightly "—your guest," she said quickly before turning back to her task.

Her confidence was all very well, but Scott wasn't convinced. Ignoring her words, he pushed on the loose boards of the fence taking the fastest route into her yard, and moved quickly to position beneath the spot on the roof where Beanie sat happily watching the commotion.

"Take it easy, little guy," he told the baby firmly. "Mama's coming to get you."

Beanie laughed and pointed a wet fist his way. "Aga, aga!" he shouted joyfully, bouncing on his diaper-padded bottom.

"No! Beanie, stay where you are!"

But the bouncing had begun him on a slow descent down the steep part of the roof. He gurgled happily as though he were sure this was part of a ride he was going to like.

"No!" A scream seemed to tear at Cathy's throat. "No, oh no!" She made a desperate lunge in his direction, but she was too late. He was in the midst of a slide toward the ground. She stared in horror as he slid away from her, terror freezing her.

But Scott's arms were there. Beanie dropped right into them. Cathy felt every bone turn to water.

"It's okay, it's okay," Scott called up to her. "I've got him."

His image swam as tears filled her eyes. "Thank God," she murmured. And Scott Bradley, she added silently.

"Can you get back inside?" he was asking anxiously. "Listen, stay where you are. I'll come up and—"

"No." She waved his suggestion aside. "I'm all right. Really. I can make it." She looked down again at the man holding her baby and she felt relief sweeping over her in a hot wave. "Just hold him. I'll be down in a minute."

Scott watched as she inched her way in through the window, then he grimaced at the child in his arms. The kid ought to be spanked. He definitely ought to be taught a lesson. It was time to be tough.

He glared at Beanie.

Beanie grinned back, his gums showing tiny teeth erupting.

"You . . . you . . . you little rascal," was the harshest Scott could do. And then he found himself grinning, too.

"Hey, listen." It was Tawny, peering over the fence with a pout. "Put that kid away and come on back, honey."

"In a minute," he said vaguely, turning as Cathy came out the sliding glass door to take Beanie from him.

"Oh, you bad little boy," she cried, holding him very tightly and closing her eyes. "What am I going to do with you?"

Scott watched. Despite everything, this was a picture that tugged at his heartstrings. The love was pure and intense. Had he ever loved anything—or anyone—like this? It was beautiful to see. What would it be like to feel?

"Hey," came the voice again from over the fence. "If you don't come back right now, I'm going to leave."

"Just a minute," Scott said without looking her way. "Is he okay?" he asked Cathy, not because he was really worried. More because he wanted to see those big blue eyes turned his way again.

Her smile was glowing. "He's fine. So fine." She gave him one last squeeze. "And so very, very bad." Dropping him gently to the ground, she gave him a pat on his well-padded rear. Then she turned back to Scott, her eyes still alight with gratitude. "I can't thank you enough for catching him that way. If you hadn't been there . . ."

Tawny's patience had worn to a tatter. "All right! All right! I'm going to leave!" she threatened from over the fence.

Scott looked at her, frowning as though it was taking him some readjusting to remember just exactly who she was. "So soon?" He shrugged. "Well, if you've gotta go, you've gotta go. Why don't you pick up a couple of those steaks on your way out? They should be about ready by now."

Fury contorted her face, and then it disappeared.

Cathy bit her lower lip to keep from laughing. "I'm sorry if I ruined your date."

He wasn't sorry at all. For some reason, the warmth of the domestic Cathy seemed much more enticing than ten sexy Tawnys could ever be. He had a momentary pang of guilt over Tawny's feelings, but it didn't last. He hadn't been any more important to her than she'd been to him. They hadn't even begun to get below surfaces. He had a feeling that an evening with Cathy would not involve anything superficial.

"Oh, it wasn't really a date," he assured Cathy. "More like an experiment."

"An experiment?"

He grinned. "Yeah. An experiment in terror."

She laughed and he watched, enjoying the way her nose wrinkled ever so slightly. "I'm glad your baby's okay," he said. "How'd he get out, anyway?"

"The latch is broken on the upstairs window in the spare bedroom. I thought I had the door closed so that he couldn't get in there. But you can't take anything for granted with a toddler around."

She said it with wry affection, not resentment, he noted. She really seemed to like her kids. Funny how he always assumed women found children a burden.

"I'll fix the latch," he offered.

"Oh." She looked surprised. "Oh, that's all right. I was going to tackle it tonight after I got the babies down."

He shrugged. "It won't take me a minute. If you've got the tools, I've got the time."

She hesitated, looking at him speculatively. If she let him into the house, she knew she would be making an admission she wasn't sure she wanted to make. But he had saved Beanie. And he was offering to do something that needed badly to be done. Memory of how she'd responded to his touch earlier that day flew through her mind, but she shook it away. She would be careful. She had to be.

"Well, thank you. That would be wonderful."

"Yeah." He took a deep breath, looking at her. "Right." Turning, he started for the front door. With the tingle of anticipation in his blood, he felt as though he were walking on air.

Four

Cathy's hand slid over Beanie's back and her fingers just barely ruffled the downy blond curls at the nape of his neck. His eyes were closed but the golden lashes still quivered slightly. He was lying in his crib. Cathy hummed softly as she touched his back, not really rubbing, just letting him know she was still there. She didn't often have time to put him to sleep this way, so right now she was giving him all of herself—her time, her attention, her love. She had a feeling he needed it right now.

The muffled sound of pounding made her lift her head and smile. Scott was working on the window across the hall. Beth and Barnaby were with him, and the triplets were, for the moment, sound asleep.

She looked down at her youngest child, so near sleep, yet still clinging to wakefulness, and love welled up in her heart. She was so lucky. All her life she'd dreamed of having a family, of being the mommy, of having rooms full of adorable children...and a strong, handsome daddy to go with them. When she was a little girl being shunted from home to home, and never feeling as if she belonged anywhere, she'd held tightly to that dream, using it to put herself to sleep every night, bringing it out to comfort herself on lonely evenings. A family. Her family.

She had the children. No one could have asked for better children, and no one could love them more than she did. That was the lucky part. The children were perfect. They filled the need she'd had all her life, filled it so well that she was truly happy, despite the fact that there was a missing piece in her dream. The part about the daddy had never worked out.

Closing her eyes, she could conjure up that mythical family. The children had looked remarkably like the three little towheads she'd ended up with. And the daddy...

Her eyes opened in shock and she gasped softly. Good Lord! The daddy of her childhood dreams had looked a lot like...a lot like...

"No," she said aloud, vehemently. Beanie stirred. Something must have happened to her memory banks. The daddy in her dream could not possibly have looked just like Scott Bradley. It was just that he was here, he was around. He was the last man she'd seen.

So, for some reason, her mind had decided to substitute his face for the daddy face. That had to be it.

There was certainly no use in trying to mold Scott Bradley into the missing piece in the picture. That was exactly what she'd done with Joey, and look how badly that had turned out. She'd learned her lesson. She would never expect any man to love her children the way she did. The man in the dream picture didn't exist, and she refused to go through life searching for something that was impossible to find.

"Aga," Beanie murmured drowsily.

"Yes, baby," she whispered, touching his golden hair. "Mama's here."

And Mama would always be there, she told herself fiercely. Mama would not get sidetracked by some handsome man; she would not let herself be tempted into a tantalizing affair with some Romeo. Scott was really very nice—and awfully attractive. And he had been there to catch Beanie. She was grateful, but she was not overwhelmed. Not at all.

When she went downstairs she would carefully, tactfully, let him know she appreciated what he had done but was not interested in a relationship of any kind. And then she would politely show him out.

She nodded, pleased with her own resolve. Yes. That was what she would do. Beanie laughed softly, though he was almost completely asleep. Cathy studied his little face carefully. He couldn't possibly be laughing at her and her hopeful plans, could he?

* * *

Scott was putting the finishing touches on the window and feeling pleased with himself. It had been some time since he'd worked with his hands this way. He'd forgotten how satisfying it could be. Fixing the window made him feel needed and necessary in the everyday world. He kind of liked that.

He wasn't sure how he felt about his audience, however. Turning his head, he looked at the two children watching his every move with solemn faces. Neither of them had said a word for ten minutes. They sat, without moving, on two chairs.

"Boo," he said softly.

Neither face changed. They looked a lot alike, both strawberry blondes, both green eyed, with freckles on their turned-up noses.

"Where did you two get that red hair?" he asked.

"From our daddy," Beth responded promptly. Barnaby didn't say a word. "Me and Barnaby look like Daddy and Beanie looks like Mommy," Beth continued earnestly.

Scott grinned at her. He had to admit he sort of liked the straightforward way she came right out with things. "Your daddy must be one good-looking guy," he offered.

Beth's face was radiant. "He is. Mommy says in college he used to smile at her and make her knees go wobbly."

Scott forced back the chuckle that rose in his throat. Cathy with wobbly knees—that was something to shoot for. He tightened the last screw and sighed with satisfaction. Beanie wouldn't be able to get out on the roof so easily next time.

Beth was still going strong in the background. "My daddy likes toast with peanut butter on it and cowboy movies," she told him solemnly. "He has a red sports car."

Scott threw her a quick smile. "He's a man after my own heart."

"Do you like kids?" she asked suddenly.

Scott turned to look at her, thrown for just a second. "Well, I...sure, I like kids," he fibbed. What else could he do?

"Daddy doesn't." She said it calmly, as though announcing the day's weather.

Scott felt a twinge of sympathy—and then regret that he couldn't come out more wholeheartedly for kids in general. Still, it wasn't good to have her think her father didn't like children. Even if it was true.

"Oh, I think you must be wrong about that," he said carefully. "I know he likes you two. And you're kids."

Beth was staring at him intently. "How do you know that? Do you know our daddy?"

The girl was too sharp for him, that was for sure. No comforting platitudes were going to mollify her. "Noooo...but..." There was no avoiding those clear green eyes. Scott cleared his throat and changed the subject just a bit. "Listen, kids. Tell me more about your daddy."

Two pairs of huge eyes stared at him.

"Why?" Beth asked softly.

He sat cross-legged on the floor closer to them. They were watching him closely, and now they both had guarded expressions. He smiled at Barnaby, and then at Beth. "Now don't get the wrong idea. I don't want you to tell me any secrets. I don't want you to say or do anything your mother wouldn't want you to do." He looked down into the little girl's eyes, trying to look sincere. "All I want to know is..." He looked from one to the other and realized he couldn't do this. They weren't adults. He couldn't question them. It was becoming more and more important to him to know if Cathy's husband still played a part in her life. But it wasn't right to ask the children. He began to wish he'd never started down this path.

He sat up straighter and shrugged. "Uh, listen, never mind. I just was wondering if I would get to meet your daddy, that's all."

"I told you," Beth said quietly. "They're divorced."

"I know." But does he come around much? That was what he wanted to know. And that was what he couldn't quite bring himself to ask.

There didn't seem to be anything left to say. Scott stared at where the toe of his shoe was sticking out from under his knee. Beth got up from her chair.

"I think I'll go down and help Mommy," she said. And then she was gone.

Scott looked at Barnaby. He got up, too, but he didn't make it out the door. Instead, he dropped behind the chair and peered out from around it, his green eyes cold as ice, as though he needed cover but was prepared to return enemy fire.

Scott stared at him for a moment, then turned back toward the window to finish his job. He had no idea what he could possibly say to this silent child that would reduce the hostility radiating from him. Maybe it was best to ignore it.

He drew the window closed and latched it, and then he heard Barnaby's voice, still coming from the vicinity of the chair. "My daddy is bigger than you," he said.

Scott looked back and managed a false smile. "Is he?"

The green eyes blinked before he fired his next salvo. "My daddy made six home runs already this year."

Scott nodded, pretending his attention was fully engaged by the job he was doing. "Good for him."

Barnaby came out from behind the chair, eyes flat and wide. "My daddy is Superman," he cried suddenly. "My daddy could beat you up." Arms raised, he made automatic weapon fire noises with his mouth as he gunned Scott down with his imaginary rifle, then turned and fled the room.

"He probably could," Scott murmured to himself, staring after the child. "I guess I'm not so tough after all." He sighed, looking at his own reflection in the full-length mirror on the opposite wall of the room. "I don't need this," he muttered to his own image. "Do I need this?"

The answer was clear. He cleaned up the evidence of his work, listening all the while to the muffled talk and movements of Cathy putting the two older children to bed. When he finally made his way downstairs, she was waiting for him.

She stood at the bottom of the stairs, looking up. She'd tied her blond hair back, but wispy curls had pulled free and now framed her face. She'd put on white slacks and a soft pink sweater, but her feet were bare. Altogether, she was the prettiest thing he'd ever seen and he had to hesitate halfway down the stairs and referee the war his emotions were going through at the sight of her.

She's gorgeous one side of the argument went. *Think how soft she'd be in your arms. Think how good her mouth would taste, how she'd melt to your touch and how those long, slender fingers would tangle in your hair, and how her body would slide beneath you and—*

She comes attached to a horde of kids, you idiot retorted the other side. *She's not alone. She's taken, body and soul, by responsibilities. You can see it on her face, read it in her eyes. She's got no time for you, and you haven't got what it takes to satisfy her need for a daddy for those kids. Give it up. Don't do something that will just make everyone involved miserable.*

Stay. See what happens.

Get out while the getting's good.

You wouldn't want to be rude.

Tell her you're expecting a long distance call.

And then he reached the bottom of the stairs and found himself within inches of her and the voices faded away, leaving him to follow his instincts. His instincts told him to smile—guardedly.

"Thank you so much," she was saying. "You've been such a help." She watched his reaction, wondering why he looked slightly wary. "I'd— Have you had any dinner?"

Whoops. That wasn't what she'd planned to say. It had just slipped out without warning. But what the heck. She owed him at least a meal after all he'd done tonight.

"Not really," he answered. "I was cooking, but dinner plans got interrupted."

Cathy nodded, remembering what he'd said to his date when he'd advised her to go on home. "I saw you go over to say goodbye to your friend before you started on the window," she said. "Did she leave you any steak?"

Scott's eyes brimmed with laughter. "Are you kidding? She took the steak, the corncobs, even the onion dip. When I got over there she had everything in a laundry basket she was 'borrowing.' I'm surprised she left me coffee for my morning meal." He grinned. "I probably ruined her plans, showing up like I did. The coffee business must nag at her. If only she'd had time to get it all!"

She found herself grinning back at him. He was cute. And she did like a man who could laugh at himself. "Serves you right," she teased.

He pretended to be taken aback, one eyebrow raised. "How so?"

Glancing over her shoulder at him, she started for the kitchen. "Like they say, you get what you pay for."

He came after her, only a step behind. "Are you implying I have to *pay* for women to date me?" he demanded.

She laughed at his outraged face. "No, silly. Of course not. But what you get out of a relationship is proportional to what you're willing to put into it." She opened the refrigerator door and leaned in. "And I have a feeling this young lady was just a name in a phone book to you when you asked her out."

"A name on a locker room wall is more like it," he muttered, leaning back against the counter and watching her trim figure as she reached for a large pot.

"What?" She straightened, placing the pot on the stove and turning on the flame.

"Nothing."

His eyes met hers and she looked away a bit too quickly, reaching for a cloth to wipe at the already spotless ceramic-tiled counter. The blond oak cabinets, the gleaming appliances, the butcher-block island, all created a setting that seemed to suit her. But he couldn't help wonder what she would look like in a little black dress with diamonds in her earlobes. He had a feeling she would be a knockout.

She put down the cloth and looked at the pot, sighing. "Well, this is going to be a letdown from steak, I'm afraid. But I fixed it for dinner and it's all I have."

She turned and found him much too close, and suddenly she realized he had the longest dark eyelashes. "I hope you like soup," she said, her voice husky.

"Soup is fine," he replied, but his gaze never left hers and though he didn't touch her, neither did he back away.

She knew they were standing too close together, knew she should move back, or say something. It was awkward to be standing here this way, but she couldn't move. It was as though there was a magnetic ring around him, and she'd gotten stuck to it.

She wanted to touch him, touch his face, smooth back his hair. He hadn't moved, hadn't said anything. Was he waiting for her to take the lead? To show him what she wanted, how much she would allow?

His eyes were dark, she couldn't read them. But she could feel the physical tug between them, the force trying to pull them together. It excited her, made her pulse beat faster. It would be so easy to sway a little, lean toward him, end up in his arms.

And in his bed. And in his life, just long enough for his leaving to break her heart. A shiver of dread passed between her shoulder blades. No! She was going to be strong. She'd gone over all the hazards, she knew them well enough by now. She wasn't going to let herself— and her family—in for that sort of anguish.

The sound of something loud and gooey making big, wet bubbles broke the spell. They both turned to look at what was on the stove, seeming to forget all about the magic that had been growing between them.

Cathy moved to turn down the heat. She lifted the lid to stir the concoction. "Your dinner calls," she said lightly.

Watching, Scott grimaced. The sounds had not been good. "What *is* that?"

She threw him an apologetic smile. "It's your soup, I'm afraid." She lifted the lid again so he could take a peek. "I hope you like split pea."

"Split pea soup?" He leaned forward and sniffed the air. "I used to love split pea soup. My mom always made it on cold winter nights."

"This was the first time I've ever made it." She pulled out a ladle and a large, deep soup bowl and began to dish it up. "Personally, I think it's horrible stuff."

Watching her, Scott became nostalgic. The scent of the soup, the steam rising from the pot all combined to bring back a wave of comfort such as he hadn't felt in a long time. "I used to love it. But nobody makes it like my mom used to. She soaked the peas for days and then threw in a huge ham bone with big hunks of ham still clinging to it."

Cathy looked up and nodded. "That's what I did."

He looked more closely. "You're kidding." He took the bowl from her and set it on the kitchen table. "This does smell good," he noted doubtfully.

She watched him, her arms folded across her chest, a smile hovering on her lips. "It looks and tastes like green slime to me," she murmured softly, waiting to hear his verdict.

He took a sip and his face relaxed in ecstasy. "Green slime! No way. Ambrosia!"

She made a face. "Ambrosia, huh? Well, I'm glad you like it." Straightening, she went to the bread box and took out a pan she'd left there. "At least these corn muffins I made to go with it are pretty good. Would you like one?"

"Corn bread?" He frowned, his spoon poised for another sip. "Don't you have any French bread?" He swallowed the soup and waved the spoon in the air. "You always eat French bread with split pea soup."

"Do you?" She shook her head, teasing him just a little. "How lucky you're here to teach me the finer points of the etiquette of split pea soup." She went back to the bread box. "You're in luck. I do have some French bread."

He didn't say a word, too busy enjoying his soup. She cut a few slices of the bread and poured him a glass of milk before sitting across from him at the kitchen table.

He took another spoonful and sighed happily. "This is wonderful. You can come cook for me anytime."

"Thanks," she said tartly, "but I'm not looking for a cooking job."

He lowered his spoon and looked at her. "That brings up an interesting point that's been bothering me," he said. "I can't believe you can really raise all these kids on babysitting money."

"You're right."

"Then what else do you do? What's your true calling?"

Her eyes got a dreamy, faraway look and she rested her chin in her hand, elbow on the tabletop. "I went to college, once upon a time, and I studied Art History. Rembrandt and El Greco and the Twentieth Century Surrealists. Got a degree and everything." She glanced back at him. "Do you have any idea how many jobs there are out there for Art History majors?"

"I haven't a clue."

"About three. And I wasn't one of the lucky trio who got them."

He nodded, not surprised. "And so you lapsed into despair and had three children to make up for it?"

"Not quite." She gave him a crooked smile. "I got married first. It seemed like a good idea at the time."

"But you are married no more."

She felt prickles of unease. This was odd, sitting here talking to him like this. He was studying her too closely, and yet she was opening up to him in a way she never did to strangers. Maybe he wasn't a stranger any longer. Maybe that was it.

"I also worked as a secretary until the twins came. And now I type medical claims for an insurance company. It's work I can do at home."

"And that's an asset, is it?"

"When you have little ones to take care of it sure is. There's no way I could pay for decent child care on the kind of salary I can command in the work force. Not until I get a bit more experience under my belt."

Scott knew she was probably right. "And the kids' father. Doesn't he . . . ?"

Send along a bit of child support? The answer was "no," but Cathy wasn't going to whine about that to Scott. She rose before he'd finished his sentence, and filled his bowl again.

"It's been a treat staying here in this big house," she said quickly, to fill the silence. "It's much bigger than our tiny apartment across town."

Scott watched as she came back to the table, murmuring thanks as she put the plate before him and sat down again. For one wild, flashing moment he had a picture of her doing the same sort of thing in his own kitchen. The image made him feel warm and toasty. But the picture quickly expanded, and suddenly there were three little faces peering from around her knees. He blinked and shook it away. He had to keep that in mind. She came with too many accessories.

"You know, this is really a strange neighborhood," she was saying. "When I was going from door to door, trying to find out if anyone knew April, it was eerie, as though everyone was living in some sort of mental ghost town. Nobody seems to know anybody else."

He shrugged and took a drink of his milk. "You know how these newer developments are," he said. "People's lives revolve around their work. Home is just a place to sleep at night."

"I guess so. It seems as much money goes into building fences as into the houses themselves."

Scott grinned at her. He was feeling good, like a cat after a meal, silky and lazy and at peace with the world. "That's the way I like it."

She shook her head. "Not me. I like the kind of place where there are no fences and everyone knows his neighbors and they have block parties and barbecues and the kids play baseball in the street."

He shuddered visibly. "Sounds terrible."

That stopped her. She leaned slowly forward, searching his eyes. "You really are a mean old man, aren't you?" she accused softly.

He pushed the plate away, full at last. "If someone who doesn't like neighborhood block parties gets that hung on him, I guess I am."

Her blue eyes searched his again. "Oh, sure," she said. "You enjoy being a grouch. But deep down, you really like kids, don't you?"

It was time to bite the bullet. There was no point in pretending. To lie to her now would be to ask for trouble. He raised his face and said it clearly. "No. Not really."

Shock widened her eyes, and then she smiled, sure he was kidding. "Oh, come on. Everybody really likes kids deep down."

He stared back, not flinching. "I don't."

She would not give up. Not wanting to be responsible, like Joey, was one thing, but to actually dislike children! That went against the laws of nature.

She gazed quizzically at him, coaxing a different response. "Think this through now," she urged. "I mean little babies in little pink bonnets with curlicues on their foreheads, with shy little grins, chubby little legs taking their first steps . . ."

He shook his head firmly. "Can't stand any of it." He leaned forward until his face was only inches from hers and said distinctly, "I think all children should be locked up in cages at birth and released on their eighteenth birthday if they've been very, very good."

She stared at him. He stared back. There was no give in him at all. This couldn't be. Not like children? Really not like them?

She took a deep breath. "Okay, I'm willing to make a concession. I know that you said you . . . don't care for children."

"Right."

"I understand that. I can come to terms with it." Why did she care? That was the question. But she didn't want to deal with that now. For some reason she had to find a way to change this answer of his. She had to find a chink in his armor.

She gazed at him, biting at her lip and thinking hard. "Okay, you say you don't like kids. But it's just because you don't know children."

He sighed, leaning back and shaking his head. "Sorry, Cathy," he said firmly, almost sad for her. "That's where you're wrong."

She hesitated. "What do you mean? I know you'd change your mind if you came to know their sweet little ways."

"You're dead wrong." He said each word emphatically.

She stared at him, completely at sea.

"Cathy, the fact of the matter is...I probably know more about children than you do."

What an odd thing to say. It didn't make any sense. She frowned, shaking her head. "What are you talking about?"

He turned in his chair, looking at her from under lowered lids. There was a storm brewing in his eyes now. For the first time, she could read his feelings in his gaze. He'd kept his tone light, but she could see the reality beneath the amused detachment. Her fingers curled around the edge of the table, as though she needed to hold on to something, as though it were going to be a bumpy ride.

"I was the oldest in a family of ten," he said. "My mother had ten children in fifteen years. I was eighteen before I escaped." His smile was humorless and he shook his head. "Until then, I was nanny to every one of my brothers and sisters. My mother's pregnancies weren't easy and she spent a lot of time in bed. Someone had to do the work. And there I was, a ready-made mother's helper. When other guys were out playing baseball, I was inside, warming formula and sterilizing bottles. I spent my days changing diapers, fixing lunch boxes, cleaning up spilled milk, when I should have been studying to get into a good college, playing football, taking out some pretty cheerleader." His grin was bittersweet. "Until I was eighteen, babies ruined my life."

Cathy felt as though the force of his bitterness had hit her physically. There was barely concealed raw emotion behind his casual attitude. She had an urge to comfort him, but she knew without being told that he would hate that right now.

"So you see," he was saying, "I know all there is to know about kids."

She nodded. "I—I'm sorry you had to go through that."

"Sorry?" His laugh sounded almost like it had before he'd started on this touchy subject. "Don't be. I learned early what some men wish they had. Better to be stuck young with a way out, than when you're older and you've made a commitment for life."

His smile was perfectly friendly, yet Cathy felt as though she'd been slapped in the face. She knew he was warning her. But she didn't feel warned. She felt challenged. She wanted to shake him, wake him up, to prove him wrong.

But there wasn't time for that now. She had other goals at the moment, other considerations to deal with. She took a deep breath and smiled back.

"But you do know what you're doing around children. So you're perfect," she said sweetly. "You're just what I need."

The wariness came back into his face. "What are you talking about?"

"Could you... would you consider taking care of some of these kids while I go to Lake Tahoe for a few days?"

Five

———

He kept his face very still, but Cathy thought she detected a flash of pure panic in his eyes. He didn't say a word, but his hands on the table spread and tensed against the butcher-block top.

"It would only be for a couple of days," she hurried to add. "I . . . I assume you won't be going out on another flight for a while. Don't you pilots get big hunks of time in between trips? I'll drive my van up. I could leave right away and be in Tahoe by noon tomorrow. Then, if I find what I'm looking for, I would be back on the road by evening."

"And when do you sleep?" he pointed out edgily.

"Oh." She thought fast. "Well, maybe I'd have to wait until the next morning to start back. But I would be back late that evening. And I could come right over and get the babies.''

''Would you?'' His eyes were glinting dangerously and his tone was sardonic at best.

''Of course I would. You'd hardly have to spend any time with them at all. Just…just two days and two and a half nights.''

''Of pure hell. Shoot, I'd do that for anyone.''

He wasn't buying, that was for sure. Cathy sighed, giving up. She was going to have to find someone else to take care of the kids while she was gone. But who? It wasn't as if she had family around or friends who didn't work.

She sat across from Scott looking wistful, her shoulders hunched, and he felt remorse. But not enough to offer to do the unthinkable. A surge of annoyance flashed through him. ''Are you going to explain to me why you're having this sudden urge to take a vacation?'' he asked evenly. ''It seems like an odd time for it.''

''Vacation?'' She stared, then realized what he meant. ''Oh, no, it's not that at all. I want to go up to Tahoe to look for April.''

''Ah.'' Well, that made it a little more understandable. But only a little. He looked at her blankly and then asked, slowly, ''Okay. I'll bite. Why Lake Tahoe?''

''I have a theory. I think she may be there, maybe even staying at the Wild Horses Casino.'' She shifted in her chair. ''You see, on Saturday evening, before I had even begun to really worry, there was a phone call.

I picked up the receiver and said 'hello.' There was no answer. But I could tell someone was on the line.''

''You think it was April.''

''At the time, that didn't occur to me. But looking back now, yes, I do think it was her. Just checking up, making sure I was here with her babies. And then, when she heard my voice, she hung up.''

Scott frowned. ''I don't get it.''

''I know. Neither do I.'' She sighed, then squared her shoulders. ''But there's no use sitting around trying to analyze why she's doing this. The thing is to find her. And there was a clue in that phone call.''

He looked skeptical. ''Really?''

She nodded. ''I could hear the jangle of slot machines in the background.''

He was becoming reluctantly intrigued now. ''Are you sure?''

''Absolutely. And as far as I know, there are only a few places near here that have slot machines.''

''Oh sure.'' His sarcasm was back. ''Las Vegas. Henderson, Laughlin, Reno—should I go on? Just about any place in Nevada.''

''Including the Nevada side of Lake Tahoe.'' She rose from her chair and gestured. ''Come on. Let me show you something.''

She led him into the living room, and using a chair as a stepladder, went up on her toes to plunge her hand deep inside a decorative urn on a high shelf.

''I honestly think April went through her entire house and obliterated everything that might give anyone a clue as to where she was going. But she forgot about these." She pulled out a handful of match-books.

Scott took a few. On each cover was printed an ad for the Wild Horses Casino. "I wonder if Tawny has this one?" he muttered.

She glanced at him but had no idea what he was talking about and decided to skip it. "Doesn't that look cluelike?" she demanded, stepping down from her perch.

"Maybe," he admitted reluctantly. He glanced up. "Have you tried calling the place and asking for her?"

She nodded. "They even tried paging her. No luck."

"Well . . ."

"But that doesn't mean anything. She could be there under a different name. And anyway, this is the only evidence of a place she might have gone to that I've found anywhere in the house. So I'd like to try it." She gave him am impish smile. "Don't you think that's a good idea?"

He regarded her balefully, still wary of her plan to dump the kids on him. "Possibly."

And it turned out his fears were justified. She took a deep breath and tried one more time. "So, will you watch the kids for me while I go up?"

He felt very selfish, but he had to refuse. "No."

"Oh." Deflated once again, she started to turn away, but he reached out to stop her, his hands taking her shoulders. She wrenched herself out of his grasp, pulling away with a jerk that surprised them both.

She stared up at him, wishing she hadn't done that. He gazed back, and only the slightest flicker in his eyes revealed that he had reacted to what she'd done. Her jerking away had been caused by doubt and disappointment, nothing more. Did he realize that? She hoped he wasn't reading too much into it. But she wasn't sure what she could do now. Apologize? No. It didn't feel right.

And anyway, he was already talking, speaking smoothly, not giving a hint that he might be offended or puzzled by her behavior.

"Cathy," he was saying softly, "I know you think I'm just being that mean old man again, but it's more than that." He shrugged in a way that managed to be manly at the same time it radiated little-boy-lost appeal. "I really don't know if I could handle having primary responsibility for your kids for any length of time. And more than that, I don't think you should go. You have no idea what April has gotten herself tangled up in. It could be dangerous."

She shook her head, her frustration plain in the strained look she threw him. "I can't just hang around here waiting," she said tightly. "I'm going crazy. That man keeps calling and I'm afraid he'll show up here."

Scott's gaze sharpened. "What man?"

She turned and flopped down into a corner of the couch, her feet pulled up close. "I told you about him. He sounds tough, kind of gangsterish. And he insists I must know where April is. He seems to want to find her in the worst way, and I can't tell if it's because he likes her or has something against her."

Scott slipped down onto the other corner of the couch, frowning. "I don't like the sound of that."

"You see why I want to get this settled? I don't know why April left, why she wants to keep her trip a secret. Is she running from this man? Why didn't she take her babies with her? Why doesn't she call to let us know she's okay? Is this guy who's calling working for the mob?" She sat huddled, full of worry, and stared at him. Wisps of corn-silk hair framed her face. "I can't just sit here any longer, waiting for something to happen! I've got to go out and make something give. I've got to."

Watching her, he felt an overwhelming desire to take her in his arms. And this time he didn't fight it. This time, he enjoyed it, letting his gaze linger on her lips, the outline of the rounded breasts beneath the pink cotton knit shirt, the long, slender legs. Looking at her, he could almost convince himself that babies weren't the minions from the netherworld he often thought them to be. More like minor annoyances. Mere gum in the works to be scraped aside at will. Whatever.

He knew he wanted to help her. She touched him. It wasn't just her beauty. There was something in her eyes, something in the way her hand reached up to push back the strands of hair that insisted on falling over those eyes. He wanted to hold her tightly and make sure nothing bad was ever said or done any-where near her. A slight shiver shook him and he gri-maced, chasing away his fanciful feelings.

"Listen," he told her. "Sit tight for tonight. In the morning, we'll make plans."

Cathy looked up. It was embarrassing to recognize that the wave of relief breaking over her was occasioned by his use of the word "we." She hadn't realized until he'd come into her life how alone she'd been with this problem. It helped just having someone else to talk it over with. But to have a partner—that was even better.

Cathy was usually an expert in the stiff upper lip department. Any woman left alone to cope with three small children had to be. And through the years, she'd done pretty well, with only the occasional good cry, something she saved for late evenings so the kids wouldn't be upset. She could handle the cards she'd been dealt.

Handling three children of her own was one thing. But adding three additional kids who weren't hers and whose mother had disappeared—that had brought her right up to the limits of her coping talents.

She had to admit it, she needed help. Any normal human being would. And right now it looked as though Scott was going to provide a bit of exactly what she needed most. The relief brought tears into her eyes and she blinked quickly, hoping he wouldn't notice.

"Great," she said, her voice husky. "Come over for breakfast and we can have a strategy session."

"Good." That husky voice cut right through him. He hesitated, knowing it was time to go home, wishing he could think of a good excuse to stay. He should go. Cathy was very tempting, but the babies and an ex-husband and a missing April—it was all getting very confusing. What could he say to her? What did he want from her? What did she want from him?

He'd always been a fairly straightforward guy. Sometimes the truth was the most effective line around. "Honesty is the best policy," he muttered fiercely.

"What?" She could tell something was going on in him but she had no idea what it could be.

He shrugged. He was probably unaware of how attractive he looked in the shadows of the lamp. "I'm going to say what I'm thinking, Cathy. You might as well know the truth."

She sat very still, not sure she was going to like this. "What is it?"

His sigh was heartrending. "I want to grab you and kiss you and you don't want me to, do you?"

Her eyes widened. "Well, at least you got that right," she responded automatically, then immediately regretted it. She knew he was remembering how she'd pulled away from his touch a few moments before. There was no way she could explain to him that her reaction had nothing to do with him or his attractiveness. To try would be to end up looking like a fool.

"I have to wonder why a nice, attractive, sexy woman like you seems to be so afraid of human contact."

Here was her chance. What could she say that wouldn't come across like a direct invitation? She tried the subtle approach. "I...I'm not afraid of human contact."

"Oh yeah?" He reached out and since she wasn't expecting it, she jumped away again. "You see what I mean?"

This was going from bad to worse. Suddenly she knew there was nothing she wanted more right now than for him to kiss her. But how to tell him so? "You startled me. That's all."

"Right."

"Really. I..." Well, what on earth could she say? "Kiss me quick, honey, and I'll prove it to you"? Hardly. She fell silent and waited.

Scott was looking moody but resigned. "It's all right," he said at last, staring into the cold, dark fireplace. "You're probably right. We're not suited to being lovers, are we? I mean, I'm not a baby person, you're crawling with babies. I'm committed to the single life-style, you're committed to making families. I love split pea soup, you hate it." He turned toward her with a lopsided grin. "Maybe we should concentrate on being friends. Okay?"

He wasn't going to kiss her. She was shocked at how sharply the disappointment cut. She hadn't realized how much the attraction she felt for him had been growing. She wanted to stop him, pull him away from this friendship business, grab hold of him while there was still time. But how could she do that without seeming too forward?

There must be a way. Other women did it. She knew all about that. She read all the magazines. The modern woman was in charge of her own destiny. She didn't settle for anything less than the best, and when the best came her way, she reached out and took it. Wow. It always sounded great in those articles. But here and now, with reality staring her in the face and Scott sitting so close beside her, it seemed next to impossible. Maybe it was just her. She didn't know how to be a modern woman.

"Friends?" she asked, her voice quavering. "Of course. Just friends." She straightened her shoulders and stiffened her pride. The last thing she wanted to do was let him know how uncertain she was. "Of course," she said again more robustly. "What else would we possibly be?"

He was gazing at her, studying her face, and there was something—was it humor?—glittering in his eyes.

"Friends," he repeated. "Yes, I think we could do that. We'll be friends."

Yes, that definitely was humor. What was he up to? "No funny business?" she asked, trying hard to keep regret out of her voice.

"Oh, hardly any." The smile was growing in his eyes. "But just to be safe, why don't we test it?"

She blinked at him. "What do you mean?"

He shrugged. "Let's try a kiss and see what happens."

"Scott!"

He was moving closer all the time. "Let it be a test of fire. We kiss and see if we can get away with no shivers, no bells. Then we'll know we're going to be just fine."

He was very close and she found she was suddenly very happy. "You're crazy," she murmured, laughing softly.

"Maybe so." He'd moved so close by now, his shoulder was right against hers. "But you know what they say. You should always humor crazy people. It keeps them calm." His arm slid around her, pulling her toward him, curling her near.

He was going to kiss her. It was going to happen. Cathy sat very still, holding her breath. A part of her, deep inside, was struggling, shouting out a warning. But she ignored it for now. No man had touched her since Joey had walked out. She'd told herself she didn't care, that she would let no man touch her ever again. Over the months, it had become easier and easier. She'd thought she'd never be tempted again. But she'd forgotten what a man could be like. Scott's hand touched her cheek and she stared into his eyes, marveling at how good he looked, and how much she wanted him to kiss her. Something warm and intoxicating was welling inside her. Was she a fool to unleash these emotions once again? Probably. But maybe it would be worth it. Just maybe.

As his hands framed her face and his mouth hovered so close to hers, she closed her eyes and waited, breathing in his breath, floating in the sense of him, hungry for just a scrap of the human contact that would let her know she was still a woman, still attractive to a man. Still alive underneath it all.

His lips barely touched hers. His hands were incredibly gentle, tracing her hairline, positioning her face so that he could make quick, stroking kisses on her lips, her eyes, the hollow at her temple. Sighing, she let herself drift. It was lovely, like a boat ride on a spring day with blossoms falling from the trees. She felt beautiful, honored, appreciated. Joey had never treated her so gently, so lovingly, especially after the children had come.

Still, she didn't feel right. Maybe Scott's embrace was too seductive. Maybe she was scared. Maybe she just wasn't ready. She didn't know herself what it was. But she drew back, gently holding Scott off. And to her relief, he didn't push it.

He sank back against the couch and looked at her, his fingers still tangled in her thick, abundant hair. He didn't want to let go. But the look in her eyes told him he would have to, so he did, slowly and reluctantly.

She was so gorgeous and she tasted so good. Everything in him ached for her. He avoided her gaze, afraid she'd read his eyes and know how much he wanted her. He didn't want to frighten her. But Lord, she was so perfect, so right for him. If only...

No, the kids were a given; they were part of her. There was no use wishing them away. It would be best to make light of the entire situation and go home. Maybe he would be able to think of something in the morning.

He turned and gave her a crooked smile. "Well, that does it. I don't think we can be just friends."

She gulped and tired to smile back. "We... we can still try to be."

He took her hand in his and played with the fingers. "Why?" he said softly. "Right now, lovers sounds so much better." He met her gaze and swore silently at himself. He should have kept his mouth shut. He could see the wariness in her face. He had to do something quickly to restore her confidence in him. "But I guess friends will have to do for now." He turned his hand in hers so that they were in the position for a handshake. "Friends it will be. Deal?"

Her smile was grateful. "Deal," she agreed.

He rose from the couch and started for the door. "You get some sleep," he told her as he went. "I'll be back for that breakfast strategy session. And we'll see where we go from there. Okay?"

"Okay."

"Goodnight."

He left, closing the door. He looked back and saw her through the window. He shook his head, perplexed. He felt so damn tender when he was with her, so protective. He could understand feeling that way about the children, but why would he feel that way toward her? It didn't make any sense. He trudged home, mulling it over.

Cathy sat very still and looked about the room as though it were all new to her. And in a way, it was. She'd just been kissed. Putting her fingers to her lips, she felt a surge of excitement. She was acting just like a teenager who'd been kissed for the very first time. Her face felt flushed. Her pulse was beating just a bit faster than normal. Had she ever reacted like this before? It had been so long, she couldn't really remember.

A kiss. What was it, after all? Just pairs of lips colliding. A gesture of affection. A question. An answer.

But what had the question been exactly? And had she found the right answer? She shivered and found herself smiling. It was all right as long as she could still smile about it, wasn't it?

Rising from the couch, she did a little dance across the living room floor, humming an old show tune. Just for this moment she was going to allow herself to be happy. Scott was handsome and fun and a genuinely nice person. She had a right to like him.

She might even have a right to love him.

"No, no, no!" she cried aloud. "Stop thinking crazy thoughts. There's no time for love, no need for it." Taking care of babies was her foremost goal, and loving Scott would only get in the way.

"So I'm not going to fall in love with you," she warned, glancing toward his house. "But I might let you kiss me again." She began to tidy things in preparation for retiring for the night. Or at least an attempt at it. She knew from experience that the triplets were probably close to waking for a midnight snack, as was their habit. Once she got them back to sleep, she would enjoy a good six hours of that herself. That is, if Beanie would let her.

On impulse, she dropped the things she'd been collecting and ran softly up the stairs to look in on the children. The triplets were sleeping like angels. Beth was lying very still, her thin arms outside the covers, her hands together as though in prayer. Barnaby was snoring lightly, his body tense even in sleep, as though he were fighting the battle of dreams and needed all his strength. And then she looked into Beanie's crib.

Two round grey eyes stared back at her. "Aga doo," he murmured.

"Oh, Beanie." She sank into the chair beside him and began to stroke his back. "Why can't you sleep, my sweetheart?"

He gave her a sleepy smile and his eyes drifted shut again.

"My precious darling," she whispered, bending down to kiss the top of his head, smelling his wonderful baby scent. A sudden wave of fierce possessiveness swept over her as she looked down at him. These children were the most important things in her life. There was no way she was going to risk hurting them by falling for that indefinable fraud called "love." No way.

She was coming back down the stairs when she heard the noise. For just a second she thought it was a mouse, or some insect trapped in the house and hurling itself against a window. Quickly she focused in on where the noise was coming from—the front door. Someone was turning a key in the lock.

She froze, clutching the banister, breath held, eyes wide. Someone was trying to get in. She watched, horrified, as the knob jiggled. Her heart was pounding so loudly now that she could no longer hear the key.

And then, suddenly the jiggling stopped. He hadn't been able to get in. She stared at the knob, strained to hear footsteps.

She never for a moment considered that it might be Scott or April, or anyone else benign. She knew right away who it was—the man on the phone. He was trying to get in and if he couldn't enter through the front door, where else might he try?

The back door. Running as softly as she could on tiptoes, she threw herself at the back door, turning the lock and slipping the bolt in place. Was it her imagination, or was there something moving in the shadows beside the house, something traveling toward . . .

The sliding glass door in the family room! Whirling, she raced across the house, flat-footed this time, not caring if she made any noise. All she wanted was to reach the sliding glass door before he did.

She made it. The bar was in place. The lock tight. She leaned against the wall, closing her eyes, breathing hard. All the doors were locked. Her babies were safe. It was time to call the police.

She turned toward the phone, but she never got there. Suddenly there was a very large man in the way.

Six

A scream rose in her throat and stuck there. He had a knife—a very large, very shiny knife. It glistened, shining in her eyes, taking away her power to act, to speak. She stared at it, transfixed. It took moments before she realized he wasn't threatening her with it. Not directly. He was cleaning it, muttering all the while.

"Damn near ruined the thing cutting that screen over the bathroom window. What'd she have to go and change the locks for anyway?"

The scream was still lodged in her throat. She stood very still, her hands covering her mouth, as though to hold the scream back. The very large man turned and scowled at her.

"You the one I've been getting on the phone all the time?" he demanded. "Where the hell is she, anyway? You can't keep hiding her. I'm going to find her sooner or later."

He was tall and hefty, his shoulders wide and strong in a sinewy way. He wore tight jeans and a fringed leather jacket. He had a tan cowboy hat pulled down low, so she couldn't see his hair, but his eyes were hazel and alert. His mouth was pulled tight in anger. And his hands kept playing with the long, sharp blade of the knife.

"Could you..." Cathy's throat was so dry, at first she couldn't get the words out. "Could you please put away that knife?" she asked hoarsely.

"What, this?" He held it up and looked from it to her. "This here's my throwing knife. It goes where I go, lady." He looked at her again, his scowl menacing. "Do you want to see me throw it? Listen. Look at this." He pretended to aim at the far wall. "I've the eye of an eagle and the hand of a hawk. You just watch this."

Cathy gasped. He wasn't pretending after all. The knife sailed through the air and landed with a crisp thunk in the center of a huge hibiscus on April's wallpaper. The handle vibrated for a moment and then went still. Cathy took a shuddering breath and put a hand out to the back of a chair to steady herself.

The man started walking over to pull his knife out. Cathy couldn't breathe properly but she felt she had to say something. "The wall...you'll...you'll ruin it."

He waved away her protest. "Oh hell, April doesn't mind. I do this all the time." He motioned with the knife as though ready to go on with more examples of his prowess.

"No!" Cathy cried. "Please, please stop it. You're making me very nervous."

He looked surprised, then disgruntled, but he put the knife away, shoving it into his belt. "Well," he demanded, looking about the room, "where is she?"

"I told you. I don't know."

The man stepped closer, threatening once again. "I said, where is she?" he growled. "And this time I want an answer."

Cathy swallowed and tried to smile, though even her lips were trembling now. "I...I think we'd better have a talk," she said, hoping he didn't notice how shaky her voice was. "Sit down, why don't you?" She gestured toward the two chairs arranged companionably with a lamp table in between them. She glanced at where the knife rested conspicuously at his hip and drew in her breath again. "Please?" she managed to say.

His heavy face darkened, but after a slight hesitation, he did as she'd suggested, sinking into the cushions with a grunt, keeping his gaze locked on her the entire time. She sat across from him. "Well?" he said impatiently. "Tell me. Where is she?"

He was just a man, she was telling herself wildly. Just a man. Even if he did throw knives and talk as if he might eat nails for breakfast. He was just a man, and a man could be talked into gentleness—sometimes. "My name is Cathy Feenstra," she tried as gingerly as one might offer a crust of bread to a lion. "Who are you?"

His rough sigh evidenced what he thought of this waste of time. "Robby Crockett," he said shortly. "Where's April?"

His glare was disconcerting, but she managed to hold her ground. "How do you know April, Mr. Crockett?" she asked, playing for time. She didn't know what she was going to do, but she knew she had to figure a way to get him out of here—or at least distracted enough so that she could call the police.

But he wasn't listening. His sharp eyes had spied something. He leaned over and reached for it on the table, and then Cathy saw what it was. The matchbook. "What's this?" he said, reading it. "Wild Horses? Lake Tahoe?" He looked up fiercely. "Don't tell me she's gone back to her old ways!" He waved the matchbook in Cathy's face.

Cathy held onto the cushion of her chair as though she were on a roller coaster ride and needed anchoring. "What do you mean?" she asked in a very small voice.

"She used to be a show girl in Las Vegas. Sure, with those long legs of hers? She was real good, real popular. She used to go out with a lot of rich men, high rollers. How do you think she got herself the nest egg to get this house?"

Cathy nodded. "Oh," she said softly.

His chest puffed out importantly. "I saved her from all that, you know. I had her working for me at my country and western club over on Pali. She's my top hostess.''

''I see.'' His top hostess. That sounded on the up-and-up. But if he was just April's employer, wondering why she wasn't coming in to work, why was he here?

''She's done this to spite me. I'm sure of that.'' His hand began to caress the knife again. ''And it's all because of those three rotten little babies. They ruined everything.''

Cathy couldn't help glancing at his hand on the knife. Watching him caress cold—and very sharp—steel made her wince. This man was not getting more gentle. In fact, thinking about the babies seemed to be riling him up.

His face was darker than ever. ''She should never have had those things in the first place. I told her so, right from the git-go. But would she listen? Hell no!''

A horrifying thought came to Cathy. What if these were his children? All kinds of possibilities flew through her mind. What if he grabbed them and held them as hostages for April's return? What if he decided he wanted to keep them? If she did call the police, they might side with him, if he claimed he was the father. She had to keep these babies away from this man, this Robby Crockett, at all costs.

She looked up and found him staring at the doorway into the hall behind her.

''Hey! What was that?'' he demanded. ''I think one of those little grasshoppers got loose.''

She swung around quickly and saw only the empty hall, leading to the stairway. "What? I don't see anything."

Robby was pointing at the doorway, waving his finger angrily. "There's some kid out there. He was making faces at me around the corner."

"What?" She turned and looked again, her heart beating, but there was absolutely nothing to see. "You must be imagining things."

Still, his reaction was beginning to worry her. She rose from the chair. "I'll just go check," she murmured, hurrying to the doorway and glancing out into the hall. There was a table and four chairs, a desk, a buffet up against the wall and a Persian carpet on the hardwood floor. There was no sign of life. The man was seeing things. Paranoid, probably. She turned to go back and bumped right into him.

He glared around the area. "Come out, you little brat," he said, his voice harsh.

Cathy's eyes suddenly caught sight of something underneath the buffet. It was Beanie's round face, his grin wide and toothless. Her heart nearly stopped in her chest.

"Let's go back, shall we?" she suggested, her voice high and shrill. She took Robby's arm and tugged. "How about a nice drink?" she said brightly, trying to edge him out of the hall and into the kitchen. "I'm sure there's something in the liquor cabinet."

She tugged again, and this time he gave a little. "Let's take a look, shall we?"

She didn't risk looking back until she had Robby in the kitchen. Then she turned and gestured wildly at her child. "Go to bed," she mouthed. "Go, now!"

Beanie laughed softly, obviously amused by the contortions she was putting her face through.

"Go!" she ordered again, pointing up the stairs. Her heart was pounding so hard she was afraid she would faint. She stepped into the kitchen quickly and closed the door, muttering a prayer.

She found him staring at her, his dark face full of suspicion. "I know what you're doing, lady," he said, his voice low but scary.

She swallowed hard and began to shake her head.

"You're trying to get me drunk, aren't you?" he went on accusingly.

She started to speak but his hand came down on her shoulder. "It won't work," he said evenly, his eyes piercing. "I came here to find April and that's what I'm going to do. If you won't tell me where she is, I'll have to try something else."

Her knees felt like rubber. "I swear," she whispered, getting desperate. "I swear I don't know where she is."

He nodded slowly, his hand still on her shoulder. "Okay. If that's the way you want to play it, I'm going to have to get rough."

Fear quivered through Cathy, tightening her throat so that she couldn't speak.

"I know what I'll do," he said softly, menacingly. "I'm going to take those babies over to my club and hold on to 'em until April decides to give me a call."

He nodded in satisfaction, a wicked smile curling his lips. "That ought to do the trick, don't you think?" He looked around the room. "Got a box or something I could carry them in?"

There was no way she was going to let him get his hands on those babies. Resolve grew in her, pushing back fear, turning her cold inside. She had to do something. Anything. She had to save them.

She glanced around the room quickly, furtively, trying to find a weapon. There was a cast iron skillet sitting on the stove, and the butcher knife in the drawer to the right of the sink. She quickly judged her chances of lunging for the knife. He was big, but if she moved fast enough...

The kitchen door creaked. They both turned to look, and there was Beanie with a wide grin, eyes alight with mischief.

Robby let out a growl and started toward him. Without thought, Cathy grabbed the huge cast iron pan and brought it down on the back of the big man's head as hard as she could, then watched in horror mixed with relief as he crumpled to the shiny vinyl floor.

Scott was having a nightmare.

He'd come home full of Cathy's scent, full of the feel of her, and he'd put his head down on his pillow sure he would dream sweet dreams of soft hands and warm, moist kisses. But he was wrong.

The bad dream had begun almost as soon as he'd closed his eyes. Tiny people had invaded his life. They clung to his legs as he tried to walk. They jumped down into his arms from trees. They hid in his cupboards and leapt out at him when he wasn't looking. They bounced across his floors. They came pouring out of his faucet when he tried to take a shower. They were everywhere, laughing and smirking and having a wonderful time at his expense.

And then they had him down, like Gulliver and the Lilliputians. Tiny ropes were binding his hands, tiny wires held back his legs, and he was struggling, trying to get away—and there was Cathy coming toward him, her arms out, and he reached for her and drew her close so that she could save him....

Suddenly he was wide awake. He lay very still, eyes open and staring at the ceiling. There wasn't a sound, and yet something was going on. He could sense it.

He slipped out of bed and went to the window to look out. The moon illuminated a ghostly figure running from the house next door toward the street. It was Cathy and she was carrying something, but he couldn't quite make out what it was, and then she disappeared around the side of the garage.

He stood there for a moment, digesting what he'd seen, and then he sprang into action, pulling on clothes as he ran down the stairs toward his front door. It never occurred to him to mind his own business. Not once.

He met her coming around the corner of the garage again and caught hold of her before she could race past him back into the house.

"Cathy, what's going on?"

She stared up at him, her eyes slightly glazed. "I'm going. I'm getting out of here. I'm taking the babies. Most of them are already in the van."

He could tell this was more than a sudden whim. "What is it? What's wrong?"

She shivered. "He came. The man from the phone calls."

"What? Where is he?"

She avoided his gaze. "Lying on the floor of the kitchen. I hit him with a frying pan."

"What?"

She looked up defiantly. "I had to. Listen, his name is Robby Crockett. He runs some club where April worked as a hostess. He's big and he's mean. He's got a knife. He threw it. He hates babies and thinks those little ones have come between him and April in some way."

Scott gave her a hard look. "I think it's time to throw in the towel and call the police, Cathy," he said quietly.

"No!" She grabbed his hand and held it tightly between her own. "We can't do that, Scott. Really, we can't. God knows what they'll do to those babies. They might even give them to Robby Crockett. He might be their father!"

Scott stared at her for a long moment. He read the intensity in her eyes, the determination in the set of her jaw. He also saw the goodness in her, the sweetness, the need to do what was right. "What can I do to help?" he asked huskily.

Her face didn't soften. She was keeping tight control in order to get through this. "Watch him. Could you? I've still got one more baby to carry down and I'm so afraid he'll wake up before I'm finished."

He nodded. "Sure. Let's go."

He followed her into the house and went straight for the kitchen. There was the large, leather-jacketed man in a heap on the floor. Though he was still breathing, he wasn't stirring.

Scott felt a wave of awareness sweep through him. He'd always thought he'd lived a pretty full life, but meeting Cathy Feenstra had added a whole new dimension to his existence. What had he done without her?

"Got any rope?" he called to her softly as she came down the stairs with the last baby.

"There's no time to look for rope," she whispered back urgently. "Besides, tying him up would be so...so premeditated, somehow." She looked at the man and shuddered. She pressed the baby she carried more tightly to her shoulder. "I just want to get out of here."

He followed her hurried progress to the van. Inside there were six car seats of various sizes, and she strapped the last baby into the empty seat, then turned to say goodbye, pulling the sliding van door shut as she did so.

"Thank you so much for all you've done, Scott," she said earnestly, her control still holding her stiff. "Could you do one last thing for me? Could you keep an eye on what happens over here—from a distance, I mean."

He was shaking his head. "No, Cathy," he said softly. "I'm afraid I can't do that."

She blinked at him worriedly. "Why not?"

He stared down at her. "Because I'm not going to be here. I'm going with you."

Relief chased disbelief out of her pretty face. "Are you sure? I thought you didn't want—"

"Forget what I said," he advised her. "Forget anything I've ever said. I want to help you. And if that means I've got to haul a van full of babies to Lake Tahoe, that's what I'll do."

She melted against him, laughing softly. "Scott." She looked up and there were tears rimming her eyes. "Oh, Scott, thank you so—"

"Don't thank me," he told her in a rough whisper. "My motives are purely selfish, believe me."

Scott released Cathy and ran back home to lock up and grab a jacket. When he returned, he noticed a strange car parked in front of April's house. A big, long, white Cadillac convertible, it had a set of long-horns on the hood, the points spread almost as wide as the car, and on the door was painted, in sparkling fluorescent orange, "Crockett Country—Sad Songs and Good Company".

"The man's car?" he asked Cathy.

She nodded and Scott made a quick stop to detach the distributor cap and throw it into the bushes. "Okay, Cathy Feenstra," he said, climbing into the driver's seat of the van. "Let's get this traveling circus on the road."

The van was old and battered, with peeling dark blue paint and a cracked back window. Cathy was used to its torn upholstery and the bench-style front seat, making getting to the rear of the vehicle when it was moving an athletic chore. But it was big and it could carry a lot, including kids and all their assorted toys, sports equipment, bicycles and everything else. They'd had three vehicles when Cathy had been married to Joey. He'd taken the Maserati, sold the Mercedes and left her old van. Others had sneered, but Cathy had always maintained he'd done her a favor. She needed the room. And now, with the three babies added to her brood, she was grateful she had it.

"Mr. Bradley is going with us, kids," she said breathlessly as she sank into the passenger's seat. She slipped on her seat belt, then looked back at the children and smiled. The three babies were asleep, but her own three were wide-eyed, watching every move. "Here we go," she told them. "Hang on."

But they weren't moving. She looked over at Scott and found him fumbling with the controls, searching for the brake, unsure of the clutch.

"How the hell do you work this thing?" he muttered impatiently.

"Do you want me to drive?" she asked. But she leaned over and pointed out the brake release.

He threw her a look and got the big vehicle moving at last. "Here we go," he said, echoing her words. "Lake Tahoe, here we come."

The engine roared to life, and they were off. Cathy glanced back at April's house. There was no angry man running out into the street, no sign that anyone knew they were leaving. And then they were out of the development and on the ramp to the freeway, and she settled back. There was no way Robby Crockett would ever guess which way they'd gone. Was there?

Seven

Though the babies continued to sleep, lulled by the movement of the van, Cathy's own children were too excited to close their eyes for the first hour of the trip. They chattered and sang songs and asked questions, until Cathy began looking at Scott covertly, wondering if they were driving him crazy. If so, there were no obvious signs of it. He even broke into a chorus of "Clementine" now and then and ended up teaching them how to sing "Found a Peanut," for which Cathy swore she would never forgive him.

"How much longer?" Beth asked four times in the next ten minutes.

"Are we there yet?" Barnaby chimed in.

A bit more of that and Cathy herself would be tear-ing her hair out. "We've got a long way to go," she told them. "You two should get some sleep."

"Will we be there when we wake up?"

Cathy shook her head. "No, I'm afraid not."

"We'll be at breakfast when you wake up," Scott interjected. "We ought to make Mammoth at about the right time, and I know someone who runs a restaurant there. How about it, you two? If you go to sleep now and don't wake up until after dawn, we'll stop for breakfast at Mammoth Lakes."

"Breakfast at a real restaurant?" Beth said with awe. "Not a fast-food place?"

Scott nodded. "It's a real restaurant, all right. With strawberry waffles and crepes and French toast with powdered sugar. Close your eyes and dream about it and when you open them, we'll be there."

Something was swelling in Cathy's chest. She wasn't sure what it was. Gratitude? Appreciation? Affection? She couldn't say. But she did know she was so glad Scott was along. He was perfect with children. How could he claim not to like them when he seemed to know just what to say, just how to act? It was such a waste!

The children began to settle down, though sleep was still going to take some time to achieve. Suddenly Barnaby leaned forward, toward his mother.

"Mommy," he said in a stage whisper as the dark night flew past, "are we being kidnapped?"

"No!" She looked quickly at Scott, then back at her son. "No, honey. It's nothing like that." She laughed softly. "Whatever gave you that idea?"

Barnaby looked at Scott, then whispered again, "He's not my daddy. Why is he driving?"

Cathy turned and took his face in her hands. "No, darling, he's not your daddy. But he's a good, good friend to our family. He's helping us." She kissed his nose. "He's helping me. Without Scott, we wouldn't be able to go to Lake Tahoe to find the babies' mother. And I'm very grateful to him. Aren't you?"

Barnaby didn't say another word, but the look he threw Scott was anything but appreciative.

They found an all-night market in San Bernardino and Cathy went in to stock up on supplies. She did raise some eyebrows when she filled her cart with enough varieties of disposable diapers to service a medium-sized day care center. She also got juices, milk, formula, apples and crackers. That would have to hold them all until the promised breakfast in Mammoth.

Scott helped her load the supplies into the van and then they were off again, cruising along the almost empty highway, heading north through the Mojave Desert. Nothing but blackness for miles and miles with their headlights making a lonely, pathetic stab at lighting the road, splitting apart the darkness. It made Cathy shiver to think how solitary their journey was.

The children were all asleep now. She knew she should sleep herself and rest up for when it would be her turn to drive. But she was still too tense, still too full of adrenaline. This was quite an adventure they were on.

"Get some sleep," Scott advised her.

She looked over at him and smiled. "I'd love to. But I can't. Not yet."

"What would help? Music?"

"No." She settled back as comfortably as she could. "Talk to me. Tell me all about yourself."

She could sense his grin rather than see it. "Oh, I see. And that will put you right to sleep, will it?"

She laughed. There was nothing better than a man with a sense of humor, a man who could joke about himself. Joey had always taken life so seriously. An outsider would have thought he was fun, always laughing and joking. What that person wouldn't have realized was that the joke was always on someone else. Joey never joked about himself. His place in life, his niche in history, was much too important, and when others didn't make the proper gestures of respect for that, his good humor quickly turned sour.

But why was she always comparing this man to Joey? She had to stop that. She knew her love for Joey was gone. The only part of it that survived lived on in these children. That she would never lose. But even the resentments had died by now. She felt sorry for Joey. He would never find what he was looking for. He didn't realize that he was searching for self-respect, and only he could provide it, not the playmates and hangers-on he ran with.

Scott seemed very different. There was a core of self-confidence about him, a satisfaction with his own personal well-being. Surely he had problems. Who didn't? But she had a feeling he was able to deal with them whenever they arose. There was a calmness to

him, a readiness to handle all that life threw at him—
even if it was a van full of babies.

But here she was, comparing them again. She had
to stop it. There was no point in it. Scott wasn't going
to be a fixture in her life. He was helping now, and he
would be gone next week. She was grateful. And she
would have fun with him while he was around. But she
had to keep in mind the fact that he would soon be
gone. She had to face facts.

So she laughed again and turned to him and was
glad they'd developed a comfortable relationship that
allowed joking. "No, silly, hearing you talk about
yourself won't put me to sleep. But it will relax me.
Tell me where you were born. Tell me where you grew
up, and what they called you when you were young."

"They called me Scotty." He looked at her and
grinned. "That's a shocker, isn't it?" He looked back
at the road and his grin faded. "And when you come
right down to it, we're headed back toward where I
grew up."

"Really?"

He nodded. "I was born and raised in Reno, Nevada. My father was the supervisor of a mining oper-
ation near there. Most of my family still lives in the
area."

She watched him in the dim light. "So your father
dug into the earth," she said softly, "and you soar in
the sky. A psychologist could have a field day with
that one."

He looked almost startled, then his face relaxed into
a slight smile. "I guess you're right. I'd never really

thought of it that way. But isn't that the way it always goes? Don't we always try for a life that's the opposite of our parents'?"

"Maybe." She was skeptical, but after all, they both were perfect examples of his theory. She'd had no family while growing up and was determined to have a wonderful one to make up for that. He'd had too much family and wanted none of it, ever again. "I don't know. I suppose if you have a happy childhood, you might want to repeat that pattern and might work to do just what your parents did to achieve it."

"Maybe. But I have yet to see evidence of that."

"You just don't know anyone with a happy childhood."

"Is that it?"

"Sure." She took a deep breath. "You just watch me and my children," she said firmly. "We'll prove it to you."

She almost made him believe it. He glanced at her, sitting so far away, and he had the urge to reach out and pull her close, so they could ride side by side like teenagers. A happy childhood. Yes, if anyone could give that to children, she probably could.

He thought of his mother. Had she started out sure that she would provide happy childhoods for all those kids? If so, something had happened along the way. He remembered her as tired and irritable all the time. The children seemed to be a tremendous burden. So why had she kept having them? That was the puzzle he would never have the answer to.

"Well, I think it's great that we'll be so near your family," Cathy was saying. "No matter what you say, you must have been a happy bunch. With so many kids in the family, how could it have been that bad?"

His laugh was humorless. "It was bad enough. My mother was sick most of the time, either with being pregnant or reactions to pregnancies. And the stress, financial and emotional, of having all those kids finally tore my parents' marriage apart."

"Oh." Cathy felt hollow and sad. "Will you get a chance to see any of them?"

He was quiet for so long, she began to wonder if he'd heard her question.

"I don't keep in touch with my family," he said at last. "In fact, most of them hate my guts."

He said it calmly, but she could sense the underlying emotions. No matter what he might pretend, rifts in a family had to hurt. "Oh no, Scott," she said quickly. "Why?"

He glanced at her again. She looked pretty by moonlight; her hair silvery, her face pale and translucent, she seemed like a porcelain figurine. Why was it that he felt he could tell her things he'd never told anyone else? Was it because she seemed to care? Because she actually seemed to listen? Or was there something more to it?

It came to him in a flash—if he didn't watch out, he could fall in love with this woman. Love. What a joke! He'd have to watch it. He'd have to be extracareful.

A cruel twist of fate, that was what it was. For the first time in his life he'd met a woman he could love.

And just for laughs, the powers that be had thrown a handful of children into the mix. Just to make things interesting. They were like that.

Well, he'd been forewarned. He was an adult now. He knew how to tally up the columns and come out with the figures. He knew what the score was, and he knew what not to do. He couldn't fall in love with Cathy. He wouldn't fall in love with her. Because to do so would be to descend into a hell he'd sworn to avoid. And so, being a smart guy, he would do all he could to avoid it.

But he could talk to her, couldn't he? He could tell her...

"I told you I had ten brothers and sisters. I was like an extra parent to them. And when I left, some of them took it rather personally. They felt betrayed." He shifted uncomfortably in his seat. "I can understand that. It took me some time to adjust to the outside world, some time to get my bearings. I didn't contact anyone at home for over two years. I was working hard, totally focused on making it. And when I finally did go home for a visit, I got the cold shoulder."

She waited, and when he didn't go on she asked, "How about the next time? How did they treat you once you were all older?"

"There was no next time. I never went back."

"Oh, Scott." Cathy felt sick. All her life, she would have done anything for a family like the one Scott had grown up in. And he'd turned his back on it, not even making an effort to get it back.

"Hey, enough about that old depressing stuff. What do I need with family, anyway? I've got friends." His grin was provocative. "Like you. We are going to get back to working on that friends business, aren't we?"

Something shivered in her as she remembered the last time they'd talked about this. But he obviously didn't take it seriously. So neither would she. "If you want."

He nodded a bit abstractedly. They slowed as they went through a tiny town that was no more than a gas station and a few windblown, fallen-down houses. They gathered speed once outside the town limits. Scott glanced at her. "If we're going to be friends, I think it's only fair that you fill me in on the facts—on where you stand with the father of those kids. Like, where he is. When he comes around. What happened."

She didn't want to do that. She was trying hard to erase Joey from her memory. Ever since she'd met Scott, it seemed Joey was hanging around the fringes of every conversation, just waiting to be invited in. "I don't think you really need my whole life story," she said stiffly.

"I didn't ask for your life story. Not yet." He pulled to the shoulder to let a sports car pass, then resumed the right lane. The van lumbered along, slow but steady.

"I can't help but think," he went on, "that the father of all those little blond mons—uh, tykes comes into the picture somewhere. Now, if we're going to be friends..."

She took a deep breath and put on a false smile. "Oh all right, friend. What do you want to know?"

"Just tell me who he is and where he is." His grin was rueful. "Barnaby's already informed me that his daddy could beat me up anytime."

Cathy's head snapped around. "What?"

"And that he's already hit six home runs. What does that mean?"

She sighed. Barnaby, her poor baby. "Their father is a professional baseball player."

Scott groaned. "I was afraid of that." He watched her face. "A real hero, huh?"

She hesitated. "Some people think so." She stopped herself. No, that wasn't fair. "I thought so, too, at one time, I have to admit. In many ways Joey—"

"Joey Feenstra?" The name had finally rung clear in Scott's head. "*The* Joey Feenstra? Plays for the New York Stars?"

She nodded.

He groaned again.

"What's the matter?"

"You've got to admit, that's pretty intimidating."

She wasn't sure she understood. "Why?"

He shook his head ruefully. "We men have a thing about sports heroes."

She knew that was true. And Joey had played it for all it was worth. "I don't know why."

"Sure you do. Even Barnaby knows it. He threw it in my face right away. He wanted me to know I wasn't as good as his dad, never could be."

She moved uncomfortably. She wasn't about to sit here and tell him, in front of the children, sleeping or not, that he was twice the man Joey Feenstra was. Even though, from what she knew of him so far, it was true.

"But who cares, anyway? There's no point to that. Who cares whether you're as good as Joey? It doesn't have anything to do with anything." She turned and looked at him. "Does it?"

He looked back, his eyes dark and enigmatic. "Of course not."

Their gazes held until Scott had to look back at the road. Cathy wasn't sure what it had meant, what had been communicated between the two of them. She only knew she was tingling and a little short of breath. She blinked hard and tried to ignore it. In a rush, she decided to tell Scott the truth.

"Well, as far as wondering if Joey's going to walk through the door any minute," she told him, her voice as low as she could manage, "you can relax. It's not a possibility."

"Oh no?"

"The kids haven't seen him in over a year. They got presents on their birthdays and at Christmas. But I think the team manager picked them out. I know it wasn't Joey's handwriting on the cards."

Scott could hear the anger in her voice. He answered softly. "Not your All-American-Greatest-Dad."

She sighed and glanced back to make sure the kids were still asleep and not overhearing this conversation. "No. In fact, the reason he left in the first place was because he couldn't handle having these children. He decided if I wanted kids, I could have them. But he wasn't going to hang around and be miserable just to make me happy. He wasn't going to live that way. So he left. I doubt if he'll ever be back."

Her voice was resigned now. He couldn't detect any lingering bitterness, except when she talked about how he'd treated his children. "That's pretty hard on the kids," he ventured, ready to draw back if she was offended by his opinion.

But she wasn't. She was open and honest now, not hiding anything. "Of course it is. It's horrible."

"How do they feel about him?"

"They still love him. What choice do they have? But he's becoming a distant figure, more and more shadowy. Barnaby has built a fantasy around him. Beth is more realistic." A smile crept into her voice. "She thinks she's going to help me find a replacement."

"Oh?"

"Didn't you notice? She's been eyeing you for the job."

Scott laughed, half-embarrassed. "Oh no. I'm trying out for Friend, not Father."

Cathy was watching his reaction. "Don't worry," she said softly. "The last thing I would ever do is marry someone who wasn't as crazy about kids as I am. I've learned my lesson."

"Good." He said the word, but something inside him wanted to say more. He wanted to protest, to claim he didn't hate children all *that* much. But he kept quiet. He glanced over and his gaze met hers and a current flashed between them. They were all alone. The children were asleep. The sky was black, the road was empty. It was only them, all alone in the universe.

"Hey," he said, his voice low and husky. "You're not getting any sleep."

"No." Her smile wavered a bit. "But I'm nice and relaxed," she claimed.

"Lie down," he ordered.

"What?"

"Put your head in my lap."

"Oh. No, I don't think—"

"Come on." He reached out and tugged her arm. "I won't bite. And I want you to get some sleep. I'm not going to last behind the wheel forever."

Suddenly she was shy. There was something so intimate about lying there with her head in his lap, her body stretched out beside him. And sleeping while he watched over her—that was some sort of ultimate in trust, wasn't it? She looked back at the children, then slowly, reluctantly, she slid down.

His jeans smelled fresh and clean and the slight roughness of the denim fabric rubbed deliciously against her cheek as she put her head down, tentatively, against his thigh.

This was impossible. She couldn't fall asleep, not here. Not touching him this way. His leg was hard and she could feel the interplay of muscles when he moved it slightly as he drove. Excitement tingled through her. She didn't remember ever being so aware of a man before. She lay very still, all she could really see was his knee, and yet she sensed him fully, his strength, his maleness.

Was she blinded by her physical reaction to him? Maybe. And yet, he was driving them to Lake Tahoe, wasn't he? He was helping her without the usual third degree, without recriminations and a lot of hurtful comments on how dumb her plan must be.

She felt his hand slip into her hair and she shuddered with a sensation of delight. His hand stilled.

"Sorry. Does this bother you?" he asked.

"No," she whispered. "No, not at all. I...I like it."

His hand moved again, gathering up her hair, caressing her softly. He looked down and almost groaned with pleasure at the sight of her. She looked so lovely. He was overcome by a wave of tenderness such as he'd never felt before. Her hair was spread out over her shoulders, over his thigh. It was like capturing an angel in his hand. He couldn't resist touching her. He couldn't help wanting her.

And he couldn't help but have fantasies. He thought of how she had tasted, and he drew in a ragged breath. Lord, his heart was beating. Could she feel it? He forced himself to breathe more slowly, easily, to control his wild pulse. He loved her being there, loved feeling her face against his thigh, loved the silk of her hair in his hand. They had to find time to be alone soon. Anticipation was getting to be an obsession with him. This drive was lasting forever.

She sighed. Her eyes were drifting shut. She'd thought when she first put her head down that she would never be able to sleep this way. He was much too male, much too exciting. But now her eyes were closing. Her legs and arms were growing heavy. She knew she was about to fall asleep. It had been a long time since she'd fallen asleep with a smile on her lips. But she did so now.

Eight

In the morning, the mood in the van was completely different from last night's. They were still thirty minutes out of Mammoth and all the children were awake—and fussing.

"I need to go to the bathroom," Barnaby said for what seemed like the hundredth time.

"We just stopped in Bishop. Can't you hold out until Mammoth?" Cathy answered.

"No!"

The babies were crying, every one of them. Cathy had crawled back, changed their diapers, dressed them in clean playsuits and given each a little of formula. But they seemed to be tired of traveling.

"They're just getting their morning exercise," Scott

told Cathy blithely. "Once they've done their forty laps, they'll quiet down."

She looked at him in amazement. How could he stay so calm? Even she was getting frazzled.

Beth had got into a whiny mood that was unusual for her. "Can't you get the babies to stop crying?" she kept complaining.

Beanie was cranky, too, sputtering and throwing away every toy Cathy tried to hand him.

"Move his seat up here next to me," Scott suggested. "It's time the two of us had a good talk."

Cathy did so, marveling again at his good humor. He hadn't had much sleep. She'd driven between Little Lake and Bishop, and he'd dozed a bit, his head on her lap this time.

It was interesting how the exchange of laps had worked out. It had put them on a much more intimate basis. She felt closer to him. His smiles were warmer, more open. Whenever she looked at him, she wanted to reach out and touch him, trail a finger across his cheek or press her palm to his temple for a second. Of course, she didn't do it. But the impulse was there.

She sat in the back and patted babies, watching Scott and Beanie interact in the front. She couldn't hear what was being said, but she could see Scott laughing, see Beanie clapping his hands and bouncing in his chair. Suddenly that childhood fantasy came back to haunt her, the one with the husband/father who looked just like Scott. He would be so perfect!

Perfect for what, her conscience demanded to know. Perfect to help you raise your children? And even if he really were perfect and willing to do it, would it be fair to the man to tie him down just for that?

Why had she married Joey? Because she'd been head over heels in love and had thought he would make her dreams come true. She'd completely brushed aside his dreams. She'd assumed they must be the same as hers, though looking back, she couldn't imagine why she might have thought so. She'd been so young. She was older now. She knew more about the world and the way it worked.

She would never again make that painful, naive mistake she'd made with Joey. Scott would make a wonderful father for her children, but he didn't want the job. So there was no use thinking about it.

In the meantime, what did Scott mean to her—just to her, with no kids involved? It was hard to think that way sometimes, hard to disengage her thinking from "kids first, me second." But there still was a person there under the Mom label. A person who would still be there when the kids were grown and gone. She really couldn't forget about that.

So the question lingered—what did Scott mean to her?

Her pulse beat quickly just thinking about it. She knew what he meant to her. He was a promise, a temptation, a seduction. His touch could bring a part of her alive that had been dormant for too long. The look in his eyes could make her blood sing. One glance at his strong, virile body could make her feel light-headed. He was enticement, a physical suggestion of fulfillment. The scent of him filled her with a delicious dread. When he was near, whispers of ecstasy tugged at her, coaxing her to turn away from "responsibility" and follow him to a temporary paradise. He was all she could ever dream of, all she must force herself to flee from.

She laughed softly to herself after that last thought, shaking her head. Boy, was she ever getting melodramatic in her old age! He was attractive, to put it simply. He was cute and she dug him. Okay?

But there was more to him than pure sensual pleasure. He was a man whom she could depend on.

He was a man she could fall in love with.

No! She mustn't even think that. It was far too dangerous.

"Here comes the Mammoth Lakes turnoff," Scott called back. "Anybody hungry?"

That brought a good response. Cathy climbed back into the front seat and found a comb to try to do something with her hair.

"What's this restaurant we're stopping at?" she asked.

"The Dutch Kitchen," he told her. "It's run by a friend of mine, Charity Ames. I went to school with her brother Mason years ago. She used to have the best restaurant in Santa Barbara before she moved to Mammoth."

"I see." Cathy looked at him sideways. "An old girlfriend?"

"Nope." He sighed heavily. "Much as I loved her cooking, she never returned the favor. I think she had a thing against anyone who was a friend of her brother's. She considered us all flakes in those days.

Anyway, I heard she's married now, with a baby and everything.''

The climb in altitude was abrupt and dramatic. Suddenly they'd left the high desert and were in the mountains. The air was crystal clear, the sky cornflower blue, and the smell of pine drifted in on cool breezes.

''Here we are.''

Scott pulled the van into the driveway of a small building designed to look like a Dutch windmill. He drove all the way around to the back of the restaurant and Cathy didn't ask why. She knew it would be best to lie low, just in case.

She turned to look at the six expectant faces behind her. ''Oh no,'' she said with a sinking feeling. ''How are we going to do this?''

''Easy,'' Scott returned cheerfully as he switched off the engine. He turned in his seat and looked at the children. ''We'll each be in charge of one little one. You take Pink. Barnaby can take Blue. Beth will take care of Daffodil. And I—'' he turned to grin at his companion in the baby seat next to him ''—I'll handle this little guy. Okay?''

There was some grumbling, but not enough to gum up the works. Cathy liked Scott's plan and appreciated not having to be the one to come up with a solution for a change. But even so, Beanie's grin of satisfaction was almost too much for her to deal with.

''Don't spoil him,'' she said under her breath to Scott.

''Why not?'' he whispered back.

She merely shook her head in exasperation and began to herd the entire brood into the restaurant. "Watch them put out the Closed sign the minute they see us coming," she said.

But that didn't happen. They'd barely made it in the door when a shriek of recognition came from the kitchen area.

"Scott Bradley! Is that really you?"

Scott turned and into his arms flew a pretty woman with wild blond hair and snapping dark eyes. "Char!" Scott said, kissing her soundly and putting her back on her feet. "Let me look at you."

She opened her arms wide, laughing. "I'm all here," she said. "But what are you doing in Mammoth?"

Scott turned to draw Cathy into the conversation. "This is Cathy Feenstra. She and I are ferrying a bunch of kids to Lake Tahoe. We may make it. We may not. But we're giving it the old college try." He grinned at the woman. "Cathy, this is Charity Ames."

"It's Carpenter now," she interjected. "I married a man named Ross Carpenter."

Scott nodded. "I heard. Where is he?"

"In Australia." She made a face. "He's got business there from time to time."

"From what I've been told, he's some highfalutin developer."

Charity grinned. "Something like that. We have a little boy, but he's at nursery school right now, or I'd let him join your crew." She smiled at Cathy, looking over the many little heads they'd brought along. "How many are there?"

"Too many," growled Scott.

"Six," supplied Cathy. "Three are mine. The others are loaners."

Charity laughed. "We've got room for you all." She called to a waitress and gave her some quick instructions.

Cathy felt right at home with the woman. She liked the way Charity and Scott interacted. There was a genuine warmth between them that could only come from years of friendship and shared experiences.

Charity turned back to them. "They'll push some tables together and round up all the high chairs. It'll only take a minute." She glanced at Scott. "You look well. Still flying?"

He nodded. "You look fantastic. I guess married life agrees with you."

"Absolutely. You ought to try it."

Scott glanced at Cathy and they both reddened, leaving Charity to gasp in astonishment. "Are you two...?"

"No," Scott said hastily. "No. We're just friends. Right, Cathy?"

She nodded vehemently. "Right. Just friends."

Charity's face took on a wise look. "I see," she said softly. "I see."

The silence stretched a little too long and all three of them tried to say something at once, leaving them laughing once again. Charity excused herself to give further instructions to her waitresses, but she was back right away.

"Listen," Scott said as she returned. "How's the rest of your family? How's your crazy sister Faith?"

Charity's look became mischievous. "Faith has a new thing." Her eyes gleamed with the deliciousness of this news. "She's selling used cars in El Paso."

Scott chuckled. "I'll bet she's the best saleswoman in the state. And how about Mason?"

"Mason's still around. He's doing some hot air ballooning in Arizona, but we expect him back about the time the first snowflake flutters down from the sky." She smiled at Cathy. "Mason is my playboy brother. He and this one here—" she gestured toward Scott "—used to tear up the town together, and land in all sorts of scrapes and expect *me* to pull their little chestnuts out of the fire."

"She exaggerates," Scott said disapprovingly. "It wasn't that way at all. We were the ones to save her skin a time or two. Remember the Arab prince who thought you were going to marry him on Valentine's Day? We had to dress you up like a circus clown to sneak you out of town."

One of the waitresses appeared and smiled at them. "We've got the table ready. Would you like to bring them in?"

Cathy turned to make sure Beth and Barnaby had their charges and they trooped into the dining area. Two tables had been pulled together. Four high chairs lined one side. Each place had a small toy or a coloring book and crayons by it. Cathy turned to Charity.

"This is lovely. But I think we'll need more chairs."

"No you won't." Charity's grin was full of mischief. "You and Scott aren't staying."

Cathy wasn't sure she'd heard right. "What?"

Another waitress appeared with a huge picnic basket. "You and Scott are having a picnic in the woods," Charity told them. "Go on. Sally will show you the way to the best picnic area around. We'll take care of the children."

Cathy was floored by the woman's generosity. "Oh no, I can't—"

"You can," she said firmly. "After the night you two have obviously had, you deserve a little pampering. Now go on, shoo. We're practically empty. It's a slow morning. On a day like this we usually don't get more than a few passing vacationers—and, of course, the local police, stopping by for doughnuts." She grinned. "We'll have fun taking care of the babies. And you'll get a nice rest." She stood on tiptoes to kiss Scott's cheek. "This is to thank you for the clown bit," she told him merrily. "Now get on with you. And don't come back for at least two hours. You hear?"

Cathy looked at Scott. He looked at her. A picnic alone in the woods. A smile began to grow between the two of them. It seemed to be inevitable. Why fight it?

Sunlight filtered down through the pines. A small crystal lake sparkled in the distance. Pine needles formed the matted bed upon which they lay. The breeze was cool, creating a whispering symphony in the tops of the trees. They were in a secluded place; no one could see them.

Remnants of their picnic lay around them. Inside the wicker basket Sally had handed them, they had found croissants, a bacon, cheese and egg quiche that had kept marvelously, coffee, orange juice, even a small bottle of champagne, two fluted glasses and a red and white checkered tablecloth with matching napkins.

They'd eaten. They'd talked. They'd touched. And now they were together, lying in one another's arms.

The "friends" theory had been discarded from the first. Neither one of them had said a word about it, but when their eyes met, they both knew. There was no way for them to be merely friends, not when electricity shimmered between them this way, not when every look, every touch, was alive with magic.

Cathy sighed, her eyes closed, and she let herself dream. What if Scott changed his mind about children? What if he became so crazy about hers that they ceased to be a problem to him? What if... he fell in love with her?

Impossible dream. That was what it was. But she couldn't keep it away.

She had a secret. She hardly even dared to tell herself. But this secret was too big to keep forever. For the second time in her life, she was very close to falling in love. She was very close to loving Scott.

She knew it was a doomed love. She probably wouldn't ever tell him about it. In some ways, that made it even more special. It was hers, and hers alone. She wouldn't let it change anything. She would make sure the children didn't suffer because of it.

She had to be careful. She didn't want it to show in her eyes. And there was also the fear that she was fooling herself. Was it just because Scott was the only man she'd been this close to since Joey had left? Was she letting a little physical attraction go to her head? She didn't want to think that, but she had to admit it was a possibility—though the more time she spent with him, the dimmer that possibility became.

Her face was pressed to Scott's chest and she could feel the thump of his heartbeat. His hand was in her hair, stroking, caressing. His long, strong body was against hers and the warmth he created was as seductive as a wood-burning fire on a frosty night. This was heaven. She'd never felt so safe and secure.

"Cathy," he murmured into her hair. "You smell like daisies look."

She lifted her face and he kissed her, gently nibbling her mouth. She parted her lips, wanting more of him, and he obliged, his tongue rasping against her in a way that inflamed her senses. She stirred, arching her body more tightly into his. If she weren't careful, she knew where this would lead. The feeling between them was explosive now. It was dangerous to tempt it. But she couldn't stop herself. She needed to feel him against her the way she needed air to breathe.

His hands rose and framed her face, holding it away so that he could look into her eyes. "Cathy," he said softly. "I want to be honest with you. Will you let me?"

Excitement was tingling through her body and she didn't want to talk. She didn't want to think. She wanted only to feel, feel him, feel them together.

She gazed at him, her vision blurred by her sensual responses. "Don't be honest," she said in return. "Don't tell me things that are good for me to hear. Don't warn me. Don't advise me. Just kiss me again."

He laughed softly and kissed her, once on her eager lips, then at the corners of her mouth. Reaching up, she wound her arms around his neck and when his mouth came near again, she captured it and enticed it to stay. The kiss went on and on. It grew from simple delight to intense pleasure, a drugging, exotic pleasure that flowered, opening in wave after wave of sensation, each more intoxicating than the last, until finally Scott drew back, and they both gasped with the need to regain their breath.

"Cathy, listen to me." He was more firm now, his voice low and rough. He took her by the shoulders and gazed intensely into her eyes. "We can't do this. Not here. Not now."

She looked up at him, her eyes wide with trust.

He groaned and tangled his hand in her hair. "I told you I want to be honest, and that's what I'm going to be." His gaze caressed her face, taking in every detail. "Cathy, I want you. I want to make love to you. I want it so badly, it's like a fire in my guts. It's driving me crazy."

She was shaking, ever so slightly. "I know," she said softly. "Scott, I know." Her hand reached up to touch his cheek and her eyes shone with her feelings.

His hand covered hers and held it to his chest. "But this isn't the right place, the right time," he went on. "I know you're vulnerable. I can tell it's been a long, long time since you've..."

She nodded and waited to hear what else he had to say.

"You've got three children, so this might sound a little odd. But...I don't think you're very experienced. Are you?"

She searched his gaze, puzzled.

He nodded. "I can tell. And much as I want you, I don't think you're ready."

Didn't he know? Couldn't he tell that she was so close to loving him? She went up on her elbow to look down at him, trailing her fingers down the cords of his neck. How could she let him know it was all right? She knew he didn't want love, not in the "forever" sense of the word. And after her knowing the man only two days, most people would have said she couldn't possibly feel that strongly yet. But she knew. She'd only been in love once before, and she was sure.

Once they got back to real life, this would fade. She knew that as surely as she knew her name. The two of them had different needs, different goals in life. Those differences would pull them apart eventually. There was no hope for a future. If they were to have anything together, it had to be now. There was no tomorrow.

Could she accept that? No, not really. But she would have to. Could she open herself to him now, give him everything she had to give, take from him all he would offer? She never would have dreamed she could do this sort of thing. It wasn't in character for her to be so hasty, so careless.

But it wasn't carelessness. She knew that. It was caring too much that drove her to want him now, to want to take a part of him with her forever.

Her fingers curled around the top button of his shirt and began to work it free. "Do you always give women this lecture?" she asked softly, her eyes shining with tamed laughter. "Or do you find me especially virginal for some reason?"

His eyebrow rose in surprise, and by the time it lowered again, she had three buttons undone and her hand was sliding inside his shirt. His dark eyes glittered. "Cathy, are you sure?"

"Sssshhhh," Leaning over him, she put a finger to his lips. If he only knew how much his concern touched her. She wasn't used to this, to having a man think of her before himself. It made her want to please him all the more. "Scott, don't worry about me. I'm a big girl. I can handle it."

He reached up and pulled her finger away so he could speak. "But Cathy, I want to make sure you understand this. I mean, you're a 'Till Death Do Us Part' sort of woman and I'm a—"

She laughed softly, easing herself on top of him, sliding to rest her hips between his legs. "Scott," she murmured, her voice low and husky, "you talk too much."

She didn't have to tell him again. His mouth sought hers and the desire that had been budding between them from the first time they had seen one another burst into bloom. His hands were moving across her back, thrusting under her sweater to loosen her bra. They explored her, journeying down to search beneath the belt of her slacks, going from the top of her backbone to her bottom, as though to claim all of her.

While his tongue seduced her mouth, his hands seduced her body, coaxing, demanding. He relished every response she gave. The cool breezes blew her hair across his face and he closed his eyes, reveling in the silken texture, the musky scent.

He murmured something. She couldn't hear the words, but she caught the tone of barely restrained passion. They rolled together, stirring up the pine needles, the crunching barely heard in the intensity of their lovemaking. Their positions had reversed, and Scott was looking down at her, his eyes smoky with his need.

He tugged aside her sweater so that her full breasts were caught by the late morning sun; the tips were dark and hard in the mountain air. His mouth was a hot flame when he leaned down to suck one, then the other. Cathy cried out and reached for him, pulling him harder against her breast, desperately needing to feel his strength.

She could feel excitement throbbing in him, but he kept it leashed, holding back to make sure she was ready. He fumbled with the closure on her slacks, and then he was peeling them down, revealing her flat stomach, her hip bones, and then the dark hair that covered his destination.

She'd never felt swept up in such a whirlwind before, never lost all sense of self the way she did now. She was nothing but passion, nothing but a burning need that had to be fulfilled. She pulled him to her, making low sounds that she could barely recognize as coming from her own throat.

He suddenly seemed weightless when he joined with her. Her body took wings. Her breathing was ragged, hard, but full of joy. He surged in her again and again and she clung to him, riding the whirlwind now, sailing into an intense ecstasy.

Spent, she lay back, panting. He lay beside her, groaning with pleasure.

"I take it back," he muttered when the ability to speak had returned to his throat. "You're definitely not virginal."

She laughed. This was what life could be like. So she laughed. Because now, at least, she'd had a taste of Eden.

Charity was waiting at the back door for their return. They'd walked up from the lake, arm in arm, carrying the picnic basket and stopping to examine rocks and mosses and clumps of lacy ferns. Scott had woven wildflowers in Cathy's hair, and she was under the happy spell of their lovemaking. But when she saw Charity's face, concern took over, blotting out contentment.

"What is it?" Even though she didn't know Charity well, she knew an expression of apprehension when she saw one. Her blood froze and fear flashed through her. "What happened? Are the children all right?"

Charity put a hand on her arm. "The children are fine. Don't worry about them. But there's been . . . a slight . . . disturbance while you were gone."

Before she could go on, the back door opened and a uniformed police officer stood in the doorway, filling it with his commanding presence. "Scott Brad-

ley?'' he asked brusquely, glaring down at Scott. ''Are
you Scott Bradley?''

Scott disentangled himself from Cathy and stood
facing the man, his legs spread, his eyes narrowed, the
picture of wary readiness. Watching, Cathy wanted to
step in between them and diffuse whatever was building here with her feminine instinct for conciliation.
''Scott,'' she whispered, reaching to touch him.
''Please.''

He ignored her, his chin lifting with masculine ar-
rogance. ''I'm Scott Bradley,'' he answered evenly.
''What's the problem, Officer?''

The man didn't answer right away. Looking down
at a piece of paper he held in his hand, he went on.
''And is this lady with you one Cathy Feenstra of
Palm Springs, California?''

''Yes.''

He looked up, staring first at one of them, then the
other. ''Are you all right, Mrs. Feenstra?'' he asked at
last.

She blinked in surprise. ''Y-yes, of course. Why
wouldn't I be?''

''We've had a report of a kidnapping. Mr. Bradley.
I'm going to have to ask you a few questions.''

For seconds, Scott and Cathy were both speech-
less, then they both tried to explain at once. The policeman put up a hand. ''Let's go inside,'' he said
sternly. ''I'd like to hear your explanations. One by
one.''

Scott entered the building, walking beside the policeman and beginning his explanation right away,

pulling out identification and talking fast. Cathy came behind with Charity.

"I've been telling Officer Mike he has it all wrong," Charity whispered as they walked into the dining area.

But Cathy wasn't listening. Her mind was wildly going over possibilities. Could Robby Crockett have called the police? What if April had tried to call after they left and, finding no one there, had contacted the cops? Somehow that had never occurred to her. Could they be technically guilty of kidnapping? After all, they had taken children they had no right to and whisked them off in the night. She wrapped her arms around herself, chilled to the bone.

The restaurant was almost empty. The officer stopped at a corner booth. Barnaby sat there all alone, his face expressionless.

"I've got the others in the room in back," Charity whispered to Cathy. "They're playing house with the babies. Sally's watching them."

Confused, Cathy went forward and gave her son a hug. Turning on the officer, she felt angry, defensive. Now that one of her children was involved, she became almost as confrontational as Scott had been in the beginning. "What is this all about?" she demanded.

The policeman nodded toward Barnaby. "He tells me he and the other kids are being kidnapped by this here Scott Bradley." He stared at Cathy, hard, as though to force the truth out of her with mind control. "What do you have to say to that?"

It took a moment for the facts to register. Barnaby had done this? Her own, sweet son? She stared at him, aghast, then looked at Scott. His face was hard, cold, his eyes resigned, but angry. He was not in the least amused.

"Oh no, Officer." She laughed, but it took a great deal of effort. "No, that's not it at all." She turned back to her son. "Barnaby, how could you? I explained what we were doing. Didn't you understand?"

The boy's face didn't change, and he didn't say a word. He obviously understood perfectly well, but had his own reasons.

Scott took her hand. "Let's talk to the officer over here, Cathy," he suggested, nodding toward the opposite corner of the room.

They went out of Barnaby's earshot and Scott quickly explained the basic circumstances of their trip—minus the information that the babies' mother was missing. "The boy's father left his mother over a year ago," he went on, squeezing Cathy's hand in apology. "Barnaby has been pretty upset about it, I think. He doesn't like to think of me in his mother's life."

Cathy glanced back at her son, full of remorse. She hadn't been paying enough attention, had she? Of course he was upset. He remembered Joey so well. And a boy his age needed a father so badly. But that sort of deprivation was hard to deal with when there was no solution in sight. So she tended to ignore it and hope it would go away. Obviously, that wasn't working.

She looked up to find Scott speaking to her. "Don't you think he probably did this to punish me for taking you off just now?" he asked.

She nodded, her huge eyes sad. "I'm sure of it." She turned to the policeman. "Officer, we're not kidnapping anyone, believe me. We're merely taking the babies to their mother in Lake Tahoe."

He stared at her for a long moment and she'd almost decided he was going to believe her when he said gruffly, "I'd like the mother's name and address, please."

Scott and Cathy exchanged glances. "Her name is April Meadows," Cathy said quickly, her heart sinking. What now? If they told him they didn't have an address for her, he would go back to his suspicions again.

"And her address," Scott was saying, "is the Wild Horses Casino, Lake Tahoe, Nevada."

Cathy's heart was beating hard. How she hoped that address was correct!

The officer wrote slowly and carefully, frowning as he jotted down the information. Cathy held her breath. Would he accept Scott's information?

Finally he looked up and nodded. "Well, your story sounds plausible," he said. "And Charity vouches for you. So I guess we can leave it at that today." He frowned harder, as though he wanted to make sure they didn't start celebrating too soon. "But I do want to warn you, if any of this data you've given me turns out to be false, I'll have to have you detained for further questioning. Do you understand?"

They nodded solemnly. The policeman tipped his hat and left the restaurant, sauntering slowly, the majesty of his power surely weighing heavy on his wide shoulders.

Scott limited his relief to a sparkle in his eyes when he gave Cathy a wink. "Go talk to your son," he told her. "I'll get the others ready."

But Barnaby wasn't talking. Cathy tried, but the more she talked, the more his lower lip protruded. Finally she put her arms around him and held him tight. "You know I love you," she said to her oldest son. "And your daddy loves you, too. He just can't be a part of our lives anymore. He can't live our way." She kissed his cheek. "But we'll be okay, you and me and Beth and Beanie. I won't ever, ever leave you. You know that, don't you?"

He turned and looked into her eyes, his gaze furtive, as though trying to see if she were telling the truth. Then he looked away again, his face as expressionless as ever.

"Ready to get back on the road?" It was Scott.

"We're ready." She let Barnaby go on ahead and put a hand on Scott's arm. "I'm sorry about what Barnaby did. I'm sure he didn't realize—"

Scott pressed his fingers to the center of her back to guide her out the door. His mouth was set in a grim line. "Kids!" was all he said, but he said it through clenched teeth.

She swallowed hard. There wasn't much point in hoping any longer, was there? It had been a foolish dream anyway. The children were bound to do something outrageous or annoying just about every day. If she had to live in fear of one of them getting into some sort of scrape, her life would become a living hell. She didn't need that. No. Things were better being left just the way they already were.

She stopped to thank Charity, who hugged her and whispered, "Good luck!" in her ear. Cathy looked at her, sure that she knew everything, and suddenly tears were welling in her eyes.

"Thanks," she said back. "But I may be beyond where luck can help me."

Squaring her shoulders, she headed out the door, the last to leave. At the corner of the building, something made her look back, and as she did, she caught sight of something in the street. It was long. It was white. It had longhorns as a hood ornament. There was Robby Crockett, and he was cruising past, looking, no doubt, for them.

Nine

There was a new urgency to their drive north now. There was no margin left for error, much less time for dawdling.

"If we'd left just two minutes sooner," Cathy kept repeating, "we would have met him coming in toward Mammoth. He would have seen us. I can't believe how close we came."

"Let's just hope he stays in town for a long lunch," Scott returned. "Otherwise, we're still in big trouble."

"How did he know to come this way? How could he have guessed?"

Scott shrugged. "Maybe he got a call from April." He grimaced. "That would be the best scenario. Just as likely, he knows her well enough to make an educated guess, just like we did." He moved restlessly behind the wheel. "I hope we find her before he does."

She glanced sideways at him, trying to study him without being obvious. She could hardly believe this was the same man she'd made love with only an hour before. His face was hard, unyielding, and when he looked at her his eyes were as unrevealing as tinted glass. There was something going on inside him. She could sense it. Emotions were tugging him in contrary directions. She had a feeling the best thing she could do was lie low until his internal war was over.

Half an hour later, the babies began to fuss. She readied herself to climb over the seat and take care of them when Scott stopped her, his hand on her shoulder.

"Send Barnaby up here next to me," he said evenly.

Cathy looked at him, biting her lip. "You won't ... hurt him?"

He stared at her, anger glimmering in his eyes. "No, Cathy," he said sarcastically. "I'll contain myself, just this once."

Of course he wouldn't hurt Barnaby. She wished she'd never said it. Still, he was angry about what had happened at the restaurant. After she'd made the adjustments, she sat in the back with the babies, her attention focused on the front seat, where Scott and Barnaby rode silently, side by side. As far as she could see, they exchanged a look now and then. But hardly a word was spoken.

Half her attention was on the road behind them, and she noticed Scott glancing in the rearview mirror a lot, as well. What would happen if Robby Crockett caught up with them? She didn't know and she hoped she wouldn't find out.

It was late afternoon when they began the long climb up into the mountains and Lake Tahoe. The sun slanted through the pines into their eyes. And then the lake was before them, blue and gorgeous.

They found the Wild Horses Casino and Hotel with little trouble. Its gaudy neon lights forming huge, raging stallions lit up the sky, even in daylight, beckoning all comers.

"Pull into the ten-minute zone," Cathy said optimistically. "I'll run in and see if she's registered here."

She kept her fingers crossed as she passed through the huge room full of chrome slot machines and green felt tables. Heading for the registration desk, she started to feel excited. If April were listed, and here, their troubles would be over.

"April Meadows?" The bored-looking clerk flipped through the registration book. "Sorry. We have no one here by that name."

"Please," Cathy put her hand out to hold the page open on the dates of the last weekend. "Could I look?" She smiled her sweetest smile and the young man frowned, but grudgingly shoved the book toward her.

"I'm not supposed to do this," he told her in a low voice. "Hurry up. If my boss sees you..."

She hurried up. There was no April, no signature that looked familiar. "Thank you." Heart sinking, she pushed the book back to the clerk and turned to start away.

"Oh!" She turned back. "She might work here. Are you sure you don't recognize the name?"

He shook his head and pointed toward the end of the hall. "Try Personnel."

"Thank you." She hurried to the door and found it slightly ajar. "Hello?" she said as she pushed it open.

Inside the little office she found two pretty, heavily made-up young women working at typewriters. They looked up expectantly as she entered.

"Hi." Her best smile got a workout again. "I'm looking for a friend. Her name is April Meadows. I thought she might be working here. Can you help me?"

"April Meadows?" one young woman repeated, shaking her head. The other pulled out a roster and ran her finger down it before saying, "Nope. Sorry. No April Meadows works here."

Cathy's gaze was riveted to the roster. She wasn't sure just why, but she had a feeling.... "Could I take a look at that list?"

The book was quickly pressed to the woman's chest. "No," she said sharply. "That's illegal. You're not allowed to see it."

Cathy looked from one to the other. Something about their attitude, something in their eyes ... Suddenly she knew they'd heard the name April Meadows before. They were holding out on her. Frustration welled inside her.

"Listen," she said, leaning forward earnestly. "I have to talk to April. It's so important. Can't you please tell me where she is?"

They both shook their heads, their faces hostile. "Sorry," said one. "Like I said, we don't know her."

Cathy sighed, straightening. She would have to come back later and try again. She turned to go, then looked back. "Well, if you do happen to run into her, will you tell her Cathy Feenstra is here? And she's got the babies." Their faces didn't change. With a shrug and a rueful smile, she left.

The afternoon was quickly turning into evening. Everyone was tired. Tempers were wearing thin. They'd tried four motels. No one would accept two adults with six children.

"There are families who really do have six children," Cathy fumed as they rode down the street, searching for yet another motel to try. "What do they do when they go on vacations?"

"They call ahead for reservations," Scott said caustically. "And then they lie."

Cathy turned to look at him. He'd been growing more and more morose. She wished she knew what she could do to fix whatever was wrong. Was it her? Or even more likely, the many, many children that came attached to her? She wasn't sure, but she wanted to find a place to stay quickly. At least then he would be able to rest.

"Why don't we try that, then?" she suggested. "Stop at a phone booth and I'll call motels. That way they won't be able to see how many children we have with us."

He was shaking his head. "I know what we have to do," he said wearily. "We should have done it from the first."

He pulled into a side street and turned the van around and started back the way they'd come. "I told you I have family up in this neck of the woods. I didn't tell you I have a sister right here in Tahoe. She and her husband run a motel. They'll give us a room."

"That's great." She left the question unspoken— why hadn't he mentioned it sooner?

But he answered anyway. "I was hoping to get through this without letting my family know I was up here." His grin was just this side of apologetic. "That was silly, of course. Margy will adore the kids. She's got about five of her own."

He pulled up before a tidy little motel of about thirty units. Though modest, it was clean and brightly painted. He turned the engine off and sat staring at the office.

"How long has it been since you last saw her?" Cathy asked.

He shook his head. "I haven't seen her since the last time I left. But she's kept in touch. She's the only one who writes to me. Every Christmas."

Cathy kept very still, letting him work out his emotions by himself. She understood now a little more of his anger, his turmoil. She'd put him in a position where he had to face things he'd managed to ignore for years. Things he would just as soon forget—that on top of too many babies. No wonder he was gloomy.

He started to unbuckle his seat belt. "Do you want me to go in with you?" she asked.

He flashed her a quick smile, then leaned over and touched her lips softly with his index finger. "Thanks," he said. "But this is something I'd better face by myself."

She watched him walk to the door of the office and go in. Sighing, she turned back to her children. Beth was playing "Here Comes the Bee" with Beanie. Barnaby was staring out the window. The three babies were squirming, getting ready to fuss again. She hoped Scott had a nice reunion with his sister. She also hoped they would all get a room for the night. She was ready to drop.

Scott returned ten minutes later, and at his side was a woman in her early thirties who looked very much like him. Cathy got out of the van to meet her.

"You're Margy," she said with a smile before anyone had a chance to introduce her. She put out her hand. "I'm Cathy Feenstra, forever in debt to your brother for all I've put him through these last two days."

Margy's answering smile was warm. She took Cathy's hand and shook it. "Scott's told me all about your problems. You must be exhausted. Come on in. We've got two empty adjoining rooms that will be perfect for your crew."

Relief buoyed them through the next hour. Scott helped change all the babies and settle them into their fresh clothes. Margy loaned them cribs and insisted on taking the dirty clothes to wash in her own machines. When they had all the children bathed and fresh-smelling again, everything seemed better.

"She's nice," Cathy said as she lounged on the bed with Pink in her arms with a bottle. She watched Scott wrestle Beanie into his jumpers.

"Who's nice?" he replied without looking up.

"Your sister. Aren't you sorry you wasted all these years?"

He looked up then, and he wasn't smiling. "I didn't waste any time at all," he said coolly. "Things happen when they're meant to happen. I'm not a family-oriented guy, Cathy. Let's both keep that in mind."

She felt properly put in her place, so she dropped the matter. But when Margy stopped in to invite them all to dinner, she gave Scott a significant smile. "See?" it said. "She's darn nice."

They ate in Margy's kitchen at a long table groaning under a mountain of food. Margy's children ranged in age from thirteen to five and they took Cathy's under their collective wing right away. Margy's husband, Sam, was a large, gruff man who looked upon his family with bemusement, as though he weren't quite sure where they'd all come from. But Margy took charge and kept things organized.

The noise level rose steadily, with squeals gaining high decibel limits, but through it all, Sam seemed merely puzzled and openly affectionate. Cathy saw that even though Scott winced now and then when a scream of laughter reached the upper ranges, he took most of the mayhem in good stride. She was proud of him.

She got up to help Margy with the dishes while the men took the children to the living room to play.

"I'm glad you and Scott have had a chance to see each other again after all this time," she said.

Margy gave her a fleeting smile. "It has been a long time," she said. "When Scotty left, I was the next in line for the job as head nanny and bottle washer."

Was there an edge in her voice? Cathy couldn't tell for sure. "I'm sure you resented his leaving."

"Yes. I did for a while." She smiled as she started the sudsy water. "But I got over it. And then I left myself, when my time came." She began scrubbing dishes and handing them to Cathy to rinse. "Once I'd gone through it myself, I lost all my bitterness toward Scotty."

Cathy hesitated, wondering if she had any right to get involved in this. After all, the things Scott had told her he'd told her reluctantly. And when you came right down to it, what did they have between them? One episode of lovemaking in the woods? A very temporary commitment to help? She felt so much for him, but she'd had no evidence he felt anything at all for her, other than physical attraction and a vague sort of friendship.

Maybe she was being too hard on herself, too hard on him. He'd warned her from the first, hadn't he? He'd never lied, never tried to hide his feelings and his lack of interest in children. If she was busy falling in love with him, it was purely her fault. It didn't give her a claim to his life, or even to discuss him with his sister.

So she hesitated. But looking at Margy's open face, hearing the affection she had for her brother in her voice, she found herself blurting things out anyway.

"Scott seems to think that his whole family hates him," she said suddenly, then looked quickly at Margy to see how she'd taken the charge. "I mean, well... maybe not 'hates' exactly..."

Margy touched her arm and shook her head, a sad smile on her face. "I have to admit, there is still some feeling of resentment in the others. They seem to think that he rejected them and it's up to him to ask to come back to the family, not up to them to beg him to do it." She shrugged. "People and their pride. You know."

Cathy nodded slowly.

Margy brightened. "But he's here now. And if I can swing it, things are going to change." She reached out and gave Cathy a hug. "So here's a big thank-you for giving me back my big brother."

Cathy laughed and hugged her back before returning to her drying job. "You know, it seems odd that Scott remembers all the hassles with the children in your family and it turns him off to having kids of his own, and yet you, who were next in line for all the chores, ended up having a big family of your own."

"It is funny, isn't it? He remembers things as being bad, I remember them as being good."

Cathy looked at her in surprise. "But...wasn't your mother sick all the time, and didn't your parents' marriage break up...?"

"Yes. That was the bad part. But there was an awful lot of good. With so many children under one roof, there had to be! There were fights and disasters and visits to the teacher for consultation. But there was also the laughter, the joy, the togetherness—the feeling of being snug in the middle of so many people who really care about you. I'll never forget that." She laughed. "And you may notice, I've tried to recreate it, to a lesser degree, right here in my own family."

"Yes, I can see that."

Margy looked at Cathy. "I want to take him home to Reno to see my mother and Jim and Frank, two brothers near our ages. Will that be all right with you?"

Cathy was stuck with her mouth open for an embarrassingly long time. "I...I...of course, but Scott doesn't ask me for permission. Margy, we barely know each other."

Margy blinked. "When did you meet?"

Cathy felt herself turning crimson. She felt like an interloper. "Night before last."

Margy stared at her, then started to laugh. "I can't believe it. The two of you seem a step away from tying the knot. To hear Scotty talk, I thought you'd been going together for ages."

Cathy grinned. "Not yet," she said, feeling cocky for no known reason. But it felt good, so she enjoyed it while it lasted.

Margy laughed and hugged her again. "You're good for him," she told her warmly. "You two stick together. You make a perfect team. I can tell."

That kind of talk gave Cathy a glow. Later, as she and Scott walked back to their rooms carrying the babies and trailing her children behind her, she said suddenly, to no one in particular, "Babies grow up."

Scott turned to her a raised eyebrow. "What?"

She took a deep breath and looked at him. "Babies grow up," she said clearly, chin high. "They're not a life sentence. They grow up and change and stop needing you so much—and then they go away."

"If you're lucky," Scott growled, but when Beanie hit his knees with a flying tackle a few seconds later, he grinned down at the bright little face and didn't seem to mind at all.

Cathy didn't say any more, but they both knew what she'd meant with her outburst. At another time, in another place, she might have been embarrassed to have been so blatant. But not now. She was beginning to feel time slipping away. She had to get in her points when she could.

They entered the adjoining motel rooms, the children rushing to the beds to jump from one to another. It was time to broach the topic of the sleeping arrangements, and right away Cathy felt awkward.

"Well, let's see," she said, avoiding Scott's gaze, "would you rather we put all male children in that room with you and all female children with me, or would you rather have the older kids and I'll take the babies?"

Scott stared at her for just a beat too long. "Is that what you want?" he asked softly.

She licked her lips, pretending not to understand the current running beneath his question. She knew what he was really asking. Are we going to be alone? Are you sorry about what happened this morning at Mammoth? Are you having second thoughts, trying to distance me?

All of the above and none of the above. She didn't know. She was too wary to force his hand. Looking about at the two twin beds in one room and the huge double bed in the other, she couldn't decide what she should do. When in doubt, play it safe. That advice whispered in her mind and she turned to smile a bright, false smile at Scott.

"How about this? You can sleep in the room with the twin beds," she suggested. "Beanie and Barnaby can share one bed, you take the other. Beth will sleep in here in the double bed with me. And we'll take the babies in their cribs."

She could see the lack of enthusiasm for her plans in his eyes. She knew what he wanted. But her children came first. He had to know that by now. "Or, we could keep the connecting door open and put the babies in the middle."

"Or pack them all out into the hallway so they'll get plenty of fresh air." His hands closed on her shoulders and he gazed down at her. "You decide, Cathy. It's up to you." He bent and kissed her, his warm mouth saying more than his words, then drew back and gazed at her. "Now while you get them settled for the night, I'm going to go back over to the Wild Horses Casino and ask about April again."

"Good idea," she said breathlessly.

"And, Cathy," he added, touching her chin with a caressing finger, "like you said a few minutes ago, babies grow up. They leave. And life goes on. If you live your life only for them, what will you have left? What will you do with the rest of your life?" His hand left her skin and he turned away. "See you in a while," he said as he left the room.

'Cathy stood where he'd left her. She was tingling with such sensational reaction to him she could hardly see straight. Her lips pulsed from his kiss. Her body yearned for his. What on earth had he set in motion? After all this time without a man, she'd thought she really didn't need that sort of thing. But he'd reawakened her. In fact, he'd found responsive areas she'd never known she had. And now his look was enough to set her off. And his touch was enough to take her straight to the edge.

It was a neat trick the way he'd turned her bit of wisdom back on her. She had to admit he had a point. But what he'd said hinted at commitments and long-term plans, and she knew he didn't mean anything of the sort. It was easy to give advice but very hard to take it.

She spent the next half hour shifting cribs and sleeping gear back and forth, trying to make up her mind how it would best suit everyone. The children grew droopier and droopier. Finally Beth came to her and said with a wide yawn. "Mommy, let all us kids stay in here with the double bed and close the door so we can go to sleep. Okay?"

Cathy hesitated. That left her with Scott and two twin beds. She cocked her head to the side and considered. Out of the mouths of babes. How simple everything seemed all of a sudden. Twin beds. No pressure. No commitment. Just twin beds in a room for two. Anything could happen—or nothing. "Well sure, Beth, if that's what you want."

Beth nodded and turned to climb into the big double bed. Her two little brothers joined her, their eyes closing before their heads hit the pillows. Cathy followed to kiss them good-night.

"Good night, Mommy," Barnaby said sleepily.

"Aga aga," Beanie agreed.

"Mommy?" Beth held her near with two little arms around her neck. "Is Scott coming back?"

"Sure he's coming back." She kissed her daughter again. "He just went out for an hour or so."

"I like him." Her eyes looked huge in the dim light. "Do you like him?"

Cathy hesitated, then tousled her daughter's hair. "Yes, baby. I like him a lot."

Beth's smile could have lit up the sky and Cathy immediately regretted having revealed how she felt about Scott. It was unfair to get Beth's hopes up. She looked down at her and thought of a hundred things she should say, a hundred warnings she should give, and ended up saying nothing at all.

"Let her hope," she told herself sadly. "It will make her happier for a while."

She stopped to check on the sleeping babies. Pink was blowing tiny baby bubbles. Blue was snoring softly, sounding like a popcorn machine. Daffodil was silent, her face peaceful and serene.

"Good night, little ones," she whispered. "Tomorrow we'll find your mother. I'm sure of it."

She closed the door between the two rooms and went into the bathroom for a long, leisurely shower. She washed her hair and rubbed on lotion when she was finished. Then she got out the heavy flannel nightgown Margy had lent her, along with a number of things for the kids, and looked at herself in the mirror. At least there was no risk of being considered seductive. The nightgown covered her from chin to toes and had a wide white yoke and ruffles at the cuffs. She looked like a Puritan, straight off the *Mayflower*. Laughing softly, she sat down to wait.

How many nights had she waited for Joey to come home? How many times had she been disappointed? And what made her think Scott would be any different? He'd left her alone with the children while he went to a casino where there were drinks and lights and dancing girls and willing women and excitement of all kinds. Why should he come back to the problems she represented? Joey had been turned off by them. Why not Scott?

But somehow she knew it wouldn't happen with Scott. He was different. That didn't mean he was hers. But it did mean he would never hurt her for no reason, as Joey had. He would do what he had to do, but he would never be malicious. With that settled in her mind, she began to drowse.

Scott felt a bit sheepish taking the teddy bears out of the van, even though it was awfully late for there to be any passersby. He was just putting the sixth furry bear into the little red wagon he'd picked up at an all-night drugstore when a party of middle-aged, late-night revellers came walking by and paused to stare at the odd picture he made.

"What have you got there?" one of them called.

Scott barely looked up. "Teddy bears."

"I can see that. Where are you taking them?"

Scott began to pull the wagon toward the motel room, but he called back casually, "Home to bed. They've lost all their savings on slot machines, poor little tykes. So I agreed to put them up for the night."

That seemed to strike them dumb, for which he was grateful. He pulled the wagon up the long walkway and into the hall, hesitating outside the door. He wasn't sure what his reception was going to be like. He wasn't sure what sort of reception he would prefer. He only knew he wanted to be with Cathy right now. Was that fair to her? Probably not. But he'd been honest from the beginning, hadn't he? She knew there was no real future for them. But there was the here and now. Lifting his hand, he rapped softly on the door.

Cathy was there in an instant, pulling the door open and looking out. The back lighting cast her hair with an angelic glow, and her eyes shone like stars. "Hi," she said, smiling a welcome that warmed his heart.

"Hi." He felt like a man coming home. Funny. He'd never really felt like that before. And here he was, coming back to a motel room where he'd never stayed.

She stepped back to let him in, glancing down at the wagon as he pulled it into the room, her eyebrows rising in surprise. "What's that you've got with you?" she asked as she closed the door.

"What, these guys?" He shrugged, looking at them sideways. "Just some old teddy bears." He sank down into the other chair and regarded her gloomily. "First it was too many babies, now too many teddy bears. I don't know which is worse."

"I see." Cathy nodded wisely, looking at the woolly creatures in the wagon, staring at her with button eyes. "Did you pick them up, or did they just follow you home?"

"A little of both." He gazed at her again, taking in the nightgown. His eyes widened. "Well, guys," he murmured out of the side of his mouth to the bears, not taking his eyes off her, "I think we came to the right place, anyway. Look. It's Mother Hubbard."

Cathy brushed aside his teasing with a shake of her head. "Tell me where you got all those bears," she insisted. "And what you're going to do with them."

He drew his brows together painfully. "It's a long story," he warned.

"I've got all night," she returned, suppressing her smile. He looked so good, his dark hair gleaming, his eyes huge in the shadows. The lines in his face took on even more distinction in the lamplight. His skin had a golden hue. She felt herself trembling in his presence. "Did you find out anything about April?"

"Only that there are people at the Wild Horses who know April Meadows. These same people will not admit it, of course. But I could tell there was something going on."

"You didn't find her." Disappointment welled in her again.

"Nope. But I talked about her a lot. And I left this address all over the place. If she is in town, I'm sure she'll hear about us. It's only a matter of time."

She bit her lips, but nodded. "And the teddy bears?" she reminded him.

"Ah, yes." He glanced down at them with a puzzled air. "They had one floor of the casino fixed up like a carnival. I can throw a mean baseball when I want to. I won two right away, and then I thought about handing out two teddy bears and leaving four little ones without and it almost broke my heart." He sighed heavily. "I had to go back and win some more."

She laughed, watching him, adoring him. "What about me?" she asked teasingly. "You only got six."

He reached into his shirt pocket. "I got you something else," he said. "I won a few hands of blackjack while making the rounds of the tables. I got you this with the winnings."

He handed her a very small box. Gingerly, she opened it. Inside was a delicate gold chain and a gold pine cone with a sprig of gold pine needles. Her thoughts went quickly back to the pine forest where they'd made love that morning and she could feel hot color rising in her cheeks. "Oh, Scott." She looked up at him, smiling her happiness.

He smiled back for only a few seconds before dropping his gaze and shifting uncomfortably in his chair. He glanced at the beds, then back at her.

"Twin beds, huh?" he noted softly.

She didn't know what to say, so she only nodded, watching him, trying to judge what he was thinking. He confused her. One minute he did something like winning the teddy bears for the children, making her wonder if he was coming around, and the next, his face closed again, shutting her out. She probably threatened him. That must be it. She could feel his affection. She could read the desire in his eyes. There were moments when she almost thought it was more, and when those moments came, she felt like racing into his arms and holding him close, blocking out everything else.

What was holding him back? Was he afraid she would want too much? Want more than he could give? And wasn't he right? Wasn't there a tiny part of her mind that was sure she could win him over, if she could only hold him tightly enough, love him passionately enough?

She closed her eyes and sighed. Twin beds. Just friends. Why not? Wasn't it safer that way?

She heard him moving and when she opened her eyes, he was standing before her, reaching for the necklace.

"Let me put it on you," he said.

She sat very still, thrilling to the brush of his fingers against her neck. He leaned close as he worked. She could feel his heat. It took her breath away.

"There." He stood back and looked at where the pine cone fell against the white yoke of the nightgown. She looked up, meeting his gaze and searching his eyes.

"Cathy..." He hesitated, not sure what she wanted him to do. He'd rarely hesitated in these situations before. But Cathy was different from any other woman he'd ever known. He didn't want to hurt her, or lose her. Funny things, scruples. Especially when you developed them at such a late age. "Cathy, I told you I was leaving the sleeping arrangements up to you, and I mean it. You're going to have to give me a road map. I'm lost."

Something clicked inside Cathy, like a switch. She needed this man. Maybe she couldn't have him forever. But she could have him for now. She rose from the chair and stood very close to him, weaving slightly.

"Scott," she said softly, her eyes shining. "Twin beds can be shoved together."

His smile was an open invitation and she walked into his arms. He began to pull her toward him, his hands caressing where they touched. "Cathy, Cathy," he whispered. "You feel like heaven."

She turned toward him, stretching her arms high to reach around his neck, and leaned into him. His hands found her breasts beneath the heavy cloth and she sighed with pleasure as he stroked them.

Her fingers flexed into his thick hair, tugging slightly. She felt warm, all her senses were alive. This was what she was made for, to love this man, to feel his body take hers, to feel her body take his.

His long fingers skillfully undid the buttons at the front of her nightgown, and then his hand slid in to touch her skin. He pulled in his breath as he looked at her, her breasts full and heavy, the nipples high and hard. He reached out to touch one with the tip of his index finger, stroking with a provocative rhythm meant to excite her.

She gasped, but she didn't pull away. Her blue eyes held his dark ones and she searched for answers, trying to read in his gaze what he really thought, really felt. Was this just to be another physical encounter? Or was it more? Were they building something, or marking time?

His mouth took hers as though in answer to her doubts. It doesn't matter, his passionate embrace told her. Nothing matters but this, the two of us here, now, taking and giving, joining together. Show me, Cathy, he seemed to be saying as his kiss became more demanding, more hungry. Show me you can forget everything else and hold me to you. Show me how much I mean to you. Convince me to stay.

For a moment his demand frightened her, and then she rose to the challenge. She could show him that. Because right now, for the moment, it was certainly true—nothing mattered but their being in each other's arms. She threw back her head and arched toward him. He swept her off her feet and laid her gently on one of the twin beds, her hair spread around her face.

Groggy with sensation, she had enough presence of mind to begin the work of unbuttoning his shirt. He helped her, shrugging away cloth, shuddering as her touch explored his chest and the hard, muscled surface of his abdomen. She fought with his belt, then his slacks, until she'd freed him. His long, shiny body was hot and alive in the lamplight.

His hands cupped her breasts, and then he leaned forward, his warm, moist mouth teasing them through the tiny holes in the lace. Sensations moved her of their own accord. She began to writhe, feeling like a woman possessed. She wanted more of him, and she moved toward him again, aching for his body.

"Cathy," he sighed, his voice almost in anguish. "I think I'm addicted to you. What am I going to do about it? What can I possibly do?"

"Love me," she whispered hotly, not even stopping to think about the double-edged sword that demand produced. "Just love me."

His touch was urgent, half with passion, half with anger. "Why did you have to come into my life?" he muttered as he pulled her fiercely against him. "Why, Cathy? Why?"

She wasn't listening to his words. She only wanted the feel of him, the smell and taste of him. His hand slipped over her ribs and flat stomach, until it rested gently between her legs. His fingers began gathering up the nightgown inch by inch.

Cathy could only stand it for so long, and then she cried out softly, her hips thrusting forward, wanting firmness. And hand met need precisely as the hem of the nightgown reached his grasp.

She shuddered with the burning ecstasy of his touch. His body came against her, taut and ready. She reached to touch him, to slide her hand along the length of him, and a sound came from her throat, so low, so hungry. She trembled.

His groan matched hers, and he writhed beneath her touch, throbbing in her hand. Her fingers tightened. "Now, Scott," she urged breathlessly. "Oh, now, please!"

She had to have him inside her, and then it was so right, so perfect, and she clung to him, clung to the feeling, wanting it to last forever, wanting him in her arms forever.

White heat, blinding, burning, cleansing. They rode it together, with tangled breaths, tangled sensations, tangled bodies, two halves of a whole.

And then they lay intertwined, hot and wet, their hearts beating fast, then slowing.

Cathy was in love. She knew it was real. There was no question in her mind. She loved this man lying here beside her. She loved him with all her heart, yet she knew that, despite the lovemaking they'd just experienced, she would never have him.

A noise startled her, and she listened intently. It was one of the triplets in the next room. She turned to kiss Scott, then started to get up.

"Where are you going?" Scott asked, lifting his head to watch her.

"One of the babies is stirring. Can't you hear it?"

He went very still. He heard it all right. Just as he'd heard it a thousand times as a boy. The cry of a baby that came before everything else. Once again he felt the familiar spasm of annoyance, the dreaded sense of obligation. He'd been kidding himself. Babies always came first. They had to. And he was a selfish pig for resenting it. But resent it he did.

Cathy knew what was going through his mind. She could feel it, as though his thoughts were hers. The baby in the next room was getting louder. With all her heart, she wanted to stay. What would happen if she just let the baby cry?

"I'm sorry, Scott," she said haltingly. "I . . . I have to go."

"Of course you do," he said. "I know that."

He was being wonderful and understanding. So why did her eyes fill with tears as she made her way to the other bedroom? Maybe she was a fool. But she'd done what she'd had to.

Ten

―――

The tension around here is as thick as pea soup,"
Margy noted when she dropped by the next morning.
She didn't understand why the mention of tension, or
of pea soup, should set Cathy off into gales of laughter, but then she didn't understand much about this
little caravan of nomadic stragglers.

The babies were whimpering. Barnaby was making
machine-gun noises from around doorways. Beth was
singing "Ten Little Monkeys Jumping on the Bed"
and acting out each part of the song. Beanie was tear-
fully clinging to Cathy as though to let her out of sight
would be the end of the world. And Scott's face
looked like a great imitation of a thundercloud.

The teddy bears had brightened the first hour of the
morning, but the glow hadn't lasted. Relations were

edgy between Scott and Cathy, and that seemed to sour everything else.

"What is going on?" Margy asked Cathy in an undertone.

Cathy had to force herself to smile. "Not a thing," she said blithely. "Just the usual chaos. I love this," she stated in a loud and very unconvincing voice while giving Scott a fierce look. "This is the way I live all the time."

Margy shook her head. "Give me a call if I can do anything to help," she said, and left quickly. Just in time, too. A customer had just driven up to park in front of the office—a man in a long white Cadillac with longhorn decorations. The license plate said California, but the decor said Texas. Margy grinned. Texans were always big spenders. She had just the room for the man.

Cathy handed Beth Daffodil and took Blue for herself. "Walk her," she advised her daughter. "Just walk her. That's all she wants."

They paced back and forth, passing each other. Pink was beginning to cry, too, but Barnaby was being too wild for Cathy to trust right now and she wasn't about to ask Scott to do anything. So she left her and continued to walk.

Watching out of the corner of her eye, Cathy saw Beanie totter on unsteady legs to where Scott was sitting and reach up to him. To his credit, Scott didn't hesitate. He reached down and helped the baby up into his lap, then stroked Beanie's head and said things to him in a voice so low that Cathy couldn't make out the words.

They looked so good together. Cathy bit her lip. There was absolutely no point in crying over spilt milk, she told herself firmly. And there was no sympathy for a woman who willfully fell in love with a man who didn't want children and then hoped, somehow, to change his mind.

What an idiot, to even let such a thought enter her head! What kind of hell would it be to live with a man who didn't really want the kids? She ought to know. She'd already gone that route. She knew what it was like to second-guess every decision. To hush the children every moment so they wouldn't bother the man in her life. To guard what was said so that he wouldn't hear about the problems, the disasters. To wait in fear for the final straw, the incident that would drive him over the edge and make him leave. Who could live like that? Who could thrive? Certainly not the children.

She glanced at Scott again, and his eyes met hers, but she couldn't read what he was thinking. She turned away, heartsick.

Suddenly the door to the motel room burst open. Cathy turned, expecting Margy, but instead, there stood Robby Crockett, big as an ox, his hand on the knife at his belt, and anger in his eyes.

Cathy gasped and held the baby close to her chest. He glared at her and sneered, "Well, I'll say this for you, girlie. You got the drop on me with that frying pan. And I do respect a woman with spunk."

Cathy whirled to look at Scott and throw him a warning glance. This was no time for macho heroics.

If he would just keep still, she might be able to save this situation. She drew her brows together, gazing beseechingly. "Don't confront him," her eyes begged.

Scott looked at her, then turned back to the man in the doorway. Every instinct he possessed said he should drive the man off of his territory. Never mind the knife. Never mind that the man was huge. This was his place and these were his dependents, and he would defend them.

But he could see Cathy's point. There were too many children around to risk having a major male confrontation. He might as well see what Cathy could come up with.

He gave her an exasperated look, then nodded slightly, letting her know they would try it her way for now.

"You double-crossin', dirty-dealin' woman," Robby was growling out. "You tricked me and you know it. Somebody's got to pay."

Cathy tried a sweet smile but he wasn't buying. She glanced at the knife and then looked away quickly. "Just calm down, Mr. Crockett," she said. "Let's be reasonable."

"I don't want reasons. I want answers. I want them, and I want them now." His eyes glittered menacingly as he lurched toward her.

Scott put Beanie on the couch and was up on his feet, moving between Cathy and Crockett in an instant. He put his arms out to protect Cathy, only to hear her begging from behind, "Please, Scott."

Taking a deep breath, he drew one hand back and left the other out as though he'd been preparing to shake hands all along. Still, he didn't move from where he stood between the two of them. "Mr. Crockett? I don't think we've met. My name's Scott Bradley."

Robby glared at the offered hand and refused to take it. "I don't know you, mister. And I don't want to know you. I don't give a damn what your name is." He turned back to scowl at Cathy. "All I want is April." He waved an accusatory finger at her. "You know where she is, don't you? I want you to take me to her."

Cathy tried to smile at the man. "Mr. Crockett, I would love to do just that." Inspiration seized her and she moved around Scott. "In fact, that's why we came up here to Lake Tahoe, to try to find her for you."

The man was slow, but not entirely gullible. "What?" he said suspiciously.

"Sure." She moved the baby from one shoulder to the other and tried to rock Pink's crib a bit with her foot at the same time, to hush her fussing. "I didn't tell you because I didn't want to get your hopes up, in case we couldn't find her. But we came roaring up here to look for her because...because we want you...and the babies..." She was groping hard for ideas. "To be reunited with April."

There. She had one. It seemed a long shot, but you never did know. Sometimes the direct approach worked. She threw a warning glance at Scott and then, eyes sparkling, she walked up to the huge cowboy and handed him Blue. "Hold this one for a minute, will you?" she said blithely. "I have to pick Pink up."

Scott went on alert, every muscle taut, ready to grab the baby back if the man started to do anything to him. But Robby Crockett seemed stunned by what Cathy had done. At first he tried to back away but the door had closed behind him and there was no place to run. She'd thrust the baby right into his arms. He had to hold it.

Hold it he did, though he had the look of a man who'd just found an alien creature crawling on his body. "Wait," he said desperately. "Wait, I don't know how to hold babies."

"There's nothing to it," Cathy said, walking away and bending down to pick Pink up. "Don't sit down! He needs to be walked."

He came toward her, trying to hand the baby back, his face stricken. "I can't do this. I never held no baby before."

"Don't be ridiculous. I saw you throw that knife. Any man who can do that can learn how to hold a baby. Here." She came up beside him. "Keep one hand behind the neck. That's great. Now put his little head against your shoulder. That's the way. You're doing fine."

He tried to do just as she said, but Blue was beginning to whimper. "He hates me," Robby cried out, like a man in pain. "They always hate me."

Cathy patted his hand comfortingly. "He doesn't hate you at all. What he hates is being ignored. Start walking and pat his little back softly at the same time. Like this." She demonstrated. He watched, his face a study in worry. Then he tried it. And in another moment, there were the two of them, pacing side by side, walking and patting. "You're doing great," Cathy told him, and in truth, Blue was quieting nicely. "You see? The baby loves you."

Scott felt a grin spreading across his face. Cathy had done it again. What a woman. Glancing down, he found Barnaby staring at him questioningly. All of Cathy's children had been watching this scene with wide eyes, not sure what to make of it, whether to be scared or amused. Barnaby was wondering how Scott fit in. Scott motioned for him to come closer.

"Hey, Barnaby," he whispered while Cathy was busy instructing Robby on burping techniques. "You ready for an assignment?"

Barnaby edged closer. "Huh?"

Scott talked out of the corner of his mouth, gangland style. "A secret mission, pal. Are you up for it?"

His eyes were wide. "Me?"

Scott nodded. "You. I need somebody small and fast and brave. What do you think?"

He still looked wary, but intrigued. Folding his arms across his chest, he pretended to stare into space. "Sure," he whispered. "I'll do it."

Scott waited as Robby made a turn near them. When he was a safe distance away, he spoke softly again. "Okay, what we need here is someone to call the cops. But I can't do it. He'll notice if I leave the room."

"He won't see me," Barnaby said, eyes alight with excitement. "I'll be too fast for him."

Scott hid a smile. "Great. You wait until he's not looking, then you sneak out and go to the office. My sister should be there. Ask her to send for the police. You got that?"

He nodded. "Yeah."

Scott touched his shoulder. "You'll be the hero, Barnaby. You'll be the one to save us all from this man."

The boy's eyes shone. He blinked rapidly. "I could. I could do it."

"You bet you could. I'm going to go over and distract him. You just wait and make sure he's looking the other way, and then you slip right out."

Barnaby looked at Scott and nodded, his little face serious. "Okay," he said, his small body tense. "Go."

Scott went. He approached the two walkers and looked the cowboy in the face. "Hey there, Mr. Robby Crockett," he said pleasantly. "Are you the father of these little babies?"

Cathy stood very still, holding her breath, one hand to her mouth.

Robby stopped and glared down at Scott. "What's it to you?" he demanded.

Scott shrugged. "Just curious, that's all. I thought I saw a definite resemblance there. In the baby boy, I mean."

Robby held out the baby he was carrying carefully and looked at him. Scott noted the faint sound of a door closing behind him. "This here's a boy?" Robby asked gruffly.

"It's a boy all right. We call him Blue. But I hear his real name is Robert."

Robby frowned, staring hard at the squirming baby. "Robert," he repeated softly.

"Now, you see what I mean, don't you?" Scott went on. "Right there, around the eyes? Spitting image of you, I'd say. What do you think, Cathy?"

Cathy came closer, looking from man to baby and back again. "You know, you're right," she said a bit breathlessly. "He looks just like his dad. That is, if you are his dad."

Robby stared at the baby a bit longer and the corners of his mouth turned up just a bit. He pressed the baby back against his shoulder, this time looking much more comfortable with the procedure. "They are cuddly little things, aren't they?"

"Sure," Cathy said, hiding her smile. "And you notice how he stopped crying once you started walking him? He knows you're his dad."

"You think so?" Awe sounded in his voice. "You think they can tell? I don't know. I haven't ever held a baby before." He let his cheek touch the top of the downy head. "I never did get this close to one before." He frowned, wonderingly. "You know, I thought they smelled bad. But this little tyke..." He took a whiff right off the top of the tiny head. "Oh man, this little one smells almost as good as April does."

Cathy's smile was radiant. "Of course. You keep them clean, use a lot of baby powder and lotion and they smell great."

"What do you know?" Robby started pacing again, his face taking on a decidedly happy look. "Hey, little baby. This here's your old man," he murmured softly as he walked.

Scott came next to Cathy and slipped an arm around her shoulders. She turned and met his gaze, and they smiled. "You're a miracle worker, lady," he whispered in her ear.

She was, wasn't she? But her smile turned ragged when she realized she hadn't been able to work that same miracle with Scott.

The door was opening again and she felt a twinge of annoyance. It was getting to be Grand Central Station around here. She turned and gave out a cry of relief. "April!"

Everyone stopped and stared at the woman in the doorway. Barnaby was with her. He looked at Scott and said, "I went, but then I saw April, so I brought her first." His little face was anxious. "Is that okay?"

Scott grinned and gave him a thumbs up. "Mission accomplished, kid," he said gruffly. "You did great."

Barnaby's face filled with pride and he sidled up to Scott, obviously prepared to stand by him in case of further need. Cathy and Robby and April were all talking at once and no one could understand a thing anyone else was saying. Scott didn't say a word. He just lounged against the connecting door, enjoying the confusion.

Finally, April took charge. Putting two fingers to her lips, she let go with an ear-piercing whistle. "You," she said, pointing at Robby, "shut up. I want to see my babies."

She sat down in a chair and Cathy handed her Pink, then got Daffodil from Beth and put her in April's lap as well. April looked up at Robby. "Do I get my little boy or not?" she demanded.

He frowned at her. "You got two of 'em. I'll hold this little fellow until you've got room on your lap. We don't want to squish 'em, do we?"

April gaped at his indignant tone and turned to Cathy. "I never," she said, shaking her head. Then she hugged her two little girls to her. "Oh, my babies, my babies, how I've missed you!"

"Some devoted mother," Robby was grumbling. "Just going off gallivanting, leaving your kids to some stranger."

April's head shot up. "I was not gallivanting. And I left them with the finest babysitter I could find." She looked at Cathy. "I'm sorry, Cathy. I know I did a rotten thing to you. But I was desperate. I couldn't find work down in Palm Springs. Trying to go looking for a job with three little babies needing me every minute was driving me crazy. But I knew the people who run the Wild Horses and I thought if I could just come up here without the kids and have some time to really go for a job here, I might have a chance. The trouble was, this one." She pointed at Robby. "I knew I couldn't let him know where I was or he'd come following me, just like he did do, didn't he?" She glared at him. "He wanted me to give up the babies and come back to work for him at his club. Which I swore I would never, never do, of course."

"You could have told me." Robby was still grumbling. "You could have let me know."

"Hah." She gave Cathy an exasperated look. "I didn't dare let him know. I didn't know what he'd do. That's why I didn't tell you where I was going." She sighed. "Cathy, I'm so sorry I did that. But I felt I had to. And I knew you could handle it. But when I tried calling you last night and no one was home . . . !''

"We were up here already, looking for you. But people at Wild Horses claimed they'd never heard of you.''

She nodded. "I'd asked them to do that, just in case Robby came looking for me. But when I went in this morning, they told me you were in town. They even knew the address.'' She hugged her babies tightly. "Which works out real well, after all. Now I don't have to run down to Palm Springs to get them.''

"What do you mean?'' Robby was being a little slow on the uptake. "You're not coming back to Palm Springs?''

She looked up at him. "I've got a job, Robby. I'm moving up here for good. It's the only place where I've been able to find work that will pay well enough to take care of me and my three little babies.''

Robby's response was to pout. "Yeah, well what about me?''

She rolled her eyes. "What about you?''

He couldn't seem to believe she didn't understand the crisis here. "I'm all alone down there.''

"Isn't that the way you said you wanted it? You didn't want to be a part of our lives. You said no babies. Babies mess things up. Well, I've got babies, Robby. So you just stay where you are and let me get on with my life.''

Robby sauntered through the room, Blue still in his arms. "Oh yeah?'' he sputtered. "Well, it seems to me you're going to need some help. I mean, what kind of a role model are you going to have for this little boy of yours without me around?''

April's eyes glittered and a strange, smug look came over her face. ''We really should go and leave these nice people alone,'' she said, gathering the babies up.

''You didn't answer me,'' Robby claimed petulantly.

She rose. ''Come on, Robby. We can discuss that in the car.''

He began to help gather things. Cathy stowed diapers into a bag, which she put in Robby's arms. Then she handed baby clothes to Scott to carry out.

All the while, Robby was still grumbling. ''And those little girls. Who's going to watch out that no guys take advantage of them when they start to date?''

Ready to go, April looked at them all with a triumphant smile. ''We'll discuss it in the car.''

He walked out, still muttering to himself. April stopped at the door and turned back to speak to Cathy. ''Thank you. I owe you big bucks. I know that. But I can't pay you right now. Can you wait until I sell my house in Palm Springs? Then I can pay you.''

Cathy didn't care much about the money any longer. It was over. Finally, the crushing responsibility of hauling the triplets all over the place was over. She felt only relief. Grinning, she waved April off. ''You just go and see if you can make Robby Crockett into Father of the Year,'' she advised her knowingly. ''Call me and let me know how things turn out.''

April grinned. ''Right. And Cathy, thanks again.''

They were gone. Scott and Cathy and the three children rattled around the two connecting rooms and looked at one another.

"It seems kind of quiet around here, doesn't it?" Scott said at last.

"It sure does." Cathy looked at him and they both began to laugh. He put his arms around her, and a moment later, Beth joined their hug, and then Beanie. Cathy looked toward the bed where Barnaby was standing. She gestured with a nod of her head. He hesitated, glancing at Scott. Scott noticed and gave him a welcoming smile. Joy leapt in Barnaby's face. Opening his arms wide, he came running toward the group and they all toppled like bowling pins, landing in a mass of bodies on the floor. A new spirit of community pervaded their little family.

"We've been through the wars together, gang," Scott told them all from his position at the bottom of the pile. "I think we all deserve to reward ourselves. How about a boat ride on the lake? Who wants to go?"

That got three little bodies off his as they all jumped up to yell, "Me! Me! Take me!" He grinned at Cathy. "How about you?"

She nodded, laughing. "Take me, too," she whispered, and he did.

For the next two days, the five of them went on vacation, hiking, swimming, boating. Margy watched the kids while Scott and Cathy spent an evening casino-hopping. They laughed in the sun. They loved under the moon. And Scott was wonderful with the children. But behind it all, Cathy knew they were merely biding time.

Nothing was said, the future was not a topic. And Scott never took back all the things he'd said about not wanting to get involved with children ever again.

Now and then she would catch him watching her, his face dark and brooding. She knew what he was thinking. She could feel that he wanted her beside him, wanted her lovemaking—but that he felt trapped by it, too. In a way, he was selling his soul to the devil. And despite all the wonderful times they had, he was not a totally happy man.

On the third day, Margy asked him to go to Reno with her to see the rest of his family. He agreed, but the look on his face was that of a man who'd heard the bell toll.

"You could come along, too," Margy told Cathy. "They'd all love to meet you."

Cathy shook her head. "No. I don't think Scott needs us along for this. It's going to be an emotional experience for him. I don't want to dilute it in any way."

Margy hugged her. "You are so good for him," she said again, as she'd said so many times. "I couldn't have picked a better match myself."

Scott was shaving when Cathy came in. She leaned against the door, watching him in the mirror. He looked back at her, his eyes troubled.

"Don't worry," she said softly. "They're going to love you."

He stared at her for a moment, then shrugged. "Maybe. But will I love them?"

He kissed her before he left, kissed her long and hard, and then turned and walked to Margy's car without a word. She watched them drive away, and then she went back into the room and began to pack. From the time they'd arrived, she'd known she would have to do this. Now the time had come.

The van was packed in less than an hour. The children were in the car seats. She looked back at the lake and tears rimmed her eyes. They'd had a wonderful time. But it was over.

She left Scott a note, telling him she would be fine driving back in the van with only her own three, thanking him for helping her with the babies, saying that she knew he could get a free flight down with almost any airline so he wasn't stranded. "Thanks again," she ended it. "It's been fun."

She left a check to cover the motel expenses, even though Margy had told her not to pay, and she left a little hostess gift for Scott's sister as well. And then she got into the van and drove off.

They made good time driving down. She broke into tears only once when they passed the Mammoth Lakes cutoff. And soon they were back in their apartment, snug in their own beds.

Their lives quickly returned to the routine they'd left when they'd gone to take care of April's triplets that weekend. Within days it was as though they'd never been away. Cathy was typing up insurance forms. The twins were learning to read. And Beanie was busy getting into everything.

Cathy thought about Scott every hour of the day. She saw his face in her mirror, she felt his touch in her dreams. And for the next week, every time the phone rang, she was sure it was going to be him.

But it never was. She told herself that was good. It was never meant to be. Better to cut it off quickly than to have their romance die a lingering death.

"Better to have loved and lost," she kept telling herself. But she didn't really believe it.

Two weeks later, April called.

"Hi, yes, it's me, I'm back in town, but just for a bit, to sign some papers. I'm flying back up this afternoon. Robby and I are getting married."

"What?"

She giggled. "Yes, things do work out, don't they? He's selling Crockett Country. He's going to open a new club in the Tahoe area. We'll be working together again. Can you believe it? The man carries those babies around with him constantly now. You can't rip them out of his arms. He's a regular nursemaid to those kids. I couldn't be happier."

"That's wonderful," Cathy said, and of course she meant it. But a tiny little part of her was asking, "But what about me? Why can't I be happy like that?"

April went on. "You've still got a lot of stuff in that house from when you stayed with the babies. You'd better come on over and clear that stuff out."

"When can I get in?"

"You've still got a key, don't you? Come on over anytime. Better make it by the first of the week, though. Oh, and Cathy, I'll be sending you a check for all you did for me very soon. Ta-ta!"

Cathy put it off for two days, but she knew she'd have to drive out to April's eventually and get it over with. She waited until a morning when Beth and Barnaby were in school, then scooped up Beanie and went.

From the moment she came down the off ramp and turned into the development, she began to get goosebumps. She drove up in front of April's house and tried not to look at Scott's next door. But she couldn't stand it. Finally, she turned, her heart in her throat. But there was nothing to see. No car. No windows open. She knew he must be gone, probably flying somewhere halfway across the world.

She should have felt relief, but instead she felt disappointment. She knew deep down she would have to see him again someday. But it looked as though this wasn't going to be that day.

She went through the house and gathered together the things she'd left behind. The whole time, her mind was going over those few days when she'd known Scott, the things they'd done together, the things they'd said. It wasn't until she had half her possessions packed into the van that she realized it had been a long time since she'd seen Beanie.

"Beanie? Beanie!" She searched the house for him. Then the yard. He was nowhere to be seen. She ran out to the street and looked up and down. No Beanie. Then she turned slowly and stared at Scott's house.

As though drawn by an invisible magnet, she walked across the lawn, ducked under the loose boards in the fence, and went into Scott's yard, past his apricot tree and the hot tub. It was then that she noticed the sliding glass door was open a few inches. Not thinking, not feeling anything, she reached out and opened it all the way, then stepped inside. There, at the kitchen table, placed high on a stack of telephone books, sat Beanie, eating a bowl of cereal and grinning from ear to ear.

"Aga doo!" he cried when he saw her, and waved his arms in the air, drops of milk spraying from his spoon.

Cathy didn't say a thing. Before she could get a word out, she saw Scott standing in the doorway into the kitchen, leaning on the frame. He was watching her, his dark eyes strangely intent.

He was gorgeous. His dark hair was just a little shaggy and a sweep of it was hanging over his eyes. He wore a blue-green shirt, open at the neck, and dark slacks. He looked tan and sexy and her head went light and fuzzy just looking at him.

She shuddered, but hid it well, and even managed a smile. "Oh, hello," she said, hoping fervently that he couldn't hear how her voice was shaking. "I see Beanie remembers you."

He nodded solemnly. "What about you, Cathy?" he said softly. "Do you remember?"

She avoided his gaze and didn't answer. "I'm glad to see you made it home all right. How was your visit to your family?"

He shifted his weight and didn't answer right away. He knew she was avoiding intimacy. "It was okay," he said at last. "I learned a lot."

"Did you?" She looked at him, searchingly. "About what?"

"About families. About not judging from appearances."

Something in his voice made her tremble again. "What do you mean, Scott?"

"I found out I had some things organized a bit wrong in my memory. For instance, here all these years I had assumed having too many babies had ruined things between my parents. From what they all tell me now, it was the babies that held the marriage together for as long as it lasted. The babies were the best thing about the relationship."

She stared at him, almost convinced he was trying to tell her something. But no. It was merely wishful thinking on her part, wasn't it? She couldn't read anything in his dark eyes. Did he still care for her? Did he hate her now? She couldn't tell.

He looked so good, but she mustn't think about that. She mustn't remember his touch or his kiss. She mustn't remember that she loved him. If she did, she would never make it through the next few minutes. She had to hold it back.

"I—I'm sorry Beanie came over to bother you."

"No problem. We've had a nice talk."

She looked up in surprise, then decided he was joking. "Oh. Well, I'm glad."

What else was there to say? I love you, Scott! Please hold me and tell me you love me, too! What would he do if she said those things? Probably start wearing garlic and hire a security guard for his home.

She turned away. She had to get out of here. "Come on, Beanie," she urged. "We have to go."

Beanie's little face took on a ferocious look. "No!" he shrieked, banging his spoon. "No, no, no!"

"His first word," Cathy said, excited. She turned to Scott. "Did you hear that? Wouldn't you know it would be 'no'?" She reached to pick him up. "Come on, Beanie. We've got to get moving."

"No, no, no!" He kicked his legs and writhed in her arms.

Cathy felt limp as a dishrag. Why now, Beanie? she moaned internally. Why do this to your mother now? "Come on, sweetie," she said aloud. "Let's go home and show off your new word to your brother and sister."

"No!" Reaching his arms toward Scott, he called out, "Dad-dy!"

Cathy gasped, staring down at her child, then turned on Scott accusingly. "You taught him to say that!"

"So what if I did?" he retorted, laughter beginning to creep into his eyes. "You ought to thank me. Some people have to hire tutors to get their babies to talk. I did it for free."

Scott had taught Beanie to call him daddy. The man who never wanted children was adopting her son. It didn't make sense. Cathy was confused. She stared at Scott. "But . . . why?"

He stared back for a moment. Beanie was still struggling in her arms, whimpering, "No, no." Scott came forward and held out his arms to the boy, who lunged for him. "Here," he said. "Let me try." He took the baby and the small arms reached for his neck.

Beanie's face was all smiles. "Dad-dy," he said lovingly. "Dad-dy."

Cathy watched in wonder. "Why?" she repeated.

He turned to look at her again and reached out to touch her hair. "Because I want to be his daddy, Cathy. I want to be the man in all your lives."

She was dreaming. She had to be. Only, this was better than her dreams ever were, because instead of imagining his arm coming around her shoulders, his breath against her cheek, his heart beating against her, here it was, in the flesh. "Scott!"

"I thought I could live without the bunch of you. I tried. I've sat here for the last two weeks in this lonely house, staring at the telephone and telling myself not to call you, that you didn't really want me in your life."

"Oh no, Scott, that's all wrong. I want you. I've never wanted anything the way I want you!"

He gazed at her fiercely, his dark eyes demanding the truth. "Are you sure, Cathy?" he asked, his voice low with emotion.

She couldn't speak. Tears of joy welled in her eyes. "Oh, Scott!"

He put Beanie down gently on the ground, then took her in his arms, kissing her with such need, such devotion, he left her breathless.

"I love you," he said, his voice ragged and rough. "Oh God, Cathy, I love you so much."

"I love you, too." She touched his face. "From the very first." Her blue eyes darkened. "But Scott, you know the children have to be my first priority. Until they're grown."

He pulled her close. "Don't worry about that. The funny thing is, I had the best time of my life being with you all on that trip to Tahoe. I learned that it isn't children that I don't like. It's being trapped. And joining your family is a choice I'm making, Cathy. No one is forcing it on me. I know exactly what I'm getting into."

"Aga doo," said a little voice from the kitchen. They looked over and saw Beanie with the cereal box in his hands, joyfully emptying the entire contents onto the floor. He looked up and grinned, waving the box at them. "Aga Dad-dy!" he improvised, and laughed.

They looked at each other and laughed, too.

"So you think you know what you're getting into, do you?" Cathy teased. "I don't think you know the half of it, mister." Her arms twined around his neck and her body molded itself to his, her eyes growing smoky with longing. "Not the half of it."

"That's exactly the way I like it," he returned, his mouth only inches from hers. "It'll be so much fun finding out the rest."

*   *   *   *   *

**A compelling novel of deadly revenge and passion
from bestselling international
romance author Penny Jordan**

Eleven years had passed but the
terror of that night was something
Pepper Minesse would never
forget. Fueled by revenge against
the four men who had brutally
shattered her past, she set in
motion a deadly plan to destroy
their futures.

Available in February!

SILHOUETTE DESIRE™

presents

AUNT EUGENIA'S TREASURES
by CELESTE HAMILTON

Liz, Cassandra and Maggie are the honored recipients of Aunt Eugenia's heirloom jewels...but Eugenia knows the real prizes are the young women themselves. Read about Aunt Eugenia's quest to find them everlasting love. Each book shines on its own, but together, they're priceless!

Available in December:
THE DIAMOND'S SPARKLE (SD #537)

Altruistic Liz Patterson wants nothing to do with Nathan Hollister, but as the fast-lane PR man tells Liz, love is something he's willing to take *very* slowly.

Available in February:
RUBY FIRE (SD #549)

Impulsive Cassandra Martin returns from her travels... ready to rekindle the flame with the man she never forgot, Daniel O'Grady.

Available in April:
THE HIDDEN PEARL (SD #561)

Cautious Maggie O'Grady comes out of her shell...and glows in the precious warmth of love when brazen Jonah Pendleton moves in next door.